HE CAME BACK

WALK THE RIGHT ROAD
BOOK 6

LORHAINNE ECKHART

Give feedback on the book at:
lorhainneeckhart@hotmail.com

Twitter: @LEckhart
Facebook: AuthorLorhainneEckhart

Printed in the U.S.A

"Emotionally intense, will leave you breathless…You will be drawn in from the beginning and won't want to stop until the very end."

DOGSMOM, REVIEWER

WALK THE RIGHT ROAD

"There was not a human emotion I did not go through while reading this book. I will forewarn you, you will need a box of tissues and a punching bag while reading this dynamic tale."

ROMANCE JUNKIES

"I loved every single book in this collection. I loved Eckhart's writing style and her ability to develop a cohesive story line around strong characters is refreshing! I am looking forward to reading more of her books."

REVIEWER CHERYL

"Lorhainne Eckhart is a master storyteller and this collection is a steal. It includes all of the books in Walk the Right Road Series."

JRA

The Choice: One Woman. Two Men. And A choice that could kill her.

Lost and Found: 'A 2013 Reader's Favorite Award Winner': A hit and run. A deserted country road. A parents worst nightmare.

Merkaba, A Novella: Everyone thought he was dead and that's exactly how he needs it to stay. Until one day he stumbles across a mysterious dark haired beauty. Only, there is nothing average or ordinary about this secretive woman, and she knows exactly what and who he is.

Bounty: *Some pasts are best forgotten.* Most cops have a past. A past, they can speak of. A past, they can share, but not for Diane.

Blown Away: The Final Chapter: Imagine that the man who's been the source of all your misery shows up on your doorstep. Imagine this man wants your forgiveness for every bad thing he's done to you and your friends. Would you believe him?

He Came Back: One woman's haunting journey when her husband returns home and everything she thought she knew about their life together has suddenly changed.

One woman's haunting journey when her husband returns home and everything she thought she knew about their life together has suddenly changed.

CHAPTER 1

Each breath he pulled deep inside his chest should have been enough for him to finally believe he was alive. Yes, he was breathing. Yes, he had all his fingers and toes. And yes, he was all in one piece. But even that physical reminder wasn't enough for Sean to really believe he was whole—or to remove the feeling that everything inside him was dead.

Sean lay on the sofa, feeling the cushions give under his weight, feeling the tension in his muscles, wound so tight he didn't think he could relax if he wanted to. He couldn't even summon rest, the absolute necessity in any person with sound reasoning. The fact was that he'd lived this way for too long: on edge, on alert, ready to jump up at a moment's notice and survive at any cost. Even though he was home now, he couldn't step out of it.

Everything had changed. He was no longer the same.

He was no longer idealistic.

Sean Robert Green had once been sheltered. He had lived comfortably and believed he knew everything. He'd been so wrong. Born in Greenville, Pennsylvania, he felt as if he'd lived a lifetime at his ripe old age of twenty-eight. How had someone who came from a small, idealistic community along the Shenango River become the mess he was now? His father, Ed, was an accountant—small time, taxes—and part-time councilman. His mother, Marion, was a homemaker, middle class with middle expectations, with three kids, two boys and a girl, each three years younger than the last. His brother, Tom, the doctor in the family, had two kids and another on the way. He was separated from his wife now and had hooked up with a nurse in Manhattan. Susan, his sister, the baby of the family, was a high-powered executive in LA with some government contracts. He didn't know what exactly she did, but she drove a Mercedes, owned a condo, and travelled extensively.

They were family, but to him they were all strangers now—all because he, the middle child that he was, had decided he needed more. He could do more. He could do better. He had joined the US military to defend his home, his family, his community. Yes, he was a hero. It was what he'd wanted in the beginning, but sometimes what we want isn't what we should have. He knew that now.

He'd made his choice, opting for life in the military, not just any part of the military but the navy, in law enforcement and security. Having Uncle Sam fund his four-year college degree and then Officer Candidate School, he thought he was saving his parents the burden of financing another child. He figured it would be exciting. He wouldn't be a grunt, on the ground, in the thick of it.

Oh, had he been wrong.

Now he was a stranger in a familiar body, moving through life, going through the motions. He squeezed his hands, fisting them so tight he could feel the moment his nails broke the skin, but that was just one more thing to cut through the numbness that filled his body, his head, his soul. Nothing could penetrate the intense horror that haunted him.

As he lay there, far from relaxed, he listened to the rustle upstairs on the second floor, the master bedroom, where his wife, Annie, slept. He knew the moment she was awake and the sound of her footsteps, knew exactly where she was and what she was doing. The toilet flushed and then water ran, and he could almost see her stopping at the door and waiting, wondering, considering. Of course she knew he wasn't there. He'd never been with her in this house, in this bed.

What was she doing? What was she thinking? She'd either come downstairs and look for him or crawl back into bed. What would she choose?

Come on, Annie. What are you doing?

He wanted his time alone, but at the same time he wanted her to walk down the stairs and come to him so he could see her face, see the innocence in her deep blue eyes, which had never seen the darkness he had. But, at the same time, he was angry. If she did see any of that darkness, it would come from him, and he didn't want that. It would be better if she weren't here at all. He wanted her away from the evil and darkness that now tainted his soul and would without a doubt kill everything good inside her. Why didn't she understand that?

The stairs creaked, and he shut his eyes, but he felt her before she stepped down the two steps into their living room, painted in soft greens and blue. Pretty, like her. It was why he'd chosen this place. Then he was watching her and how she looked in pajama shorts and a T-shirt, her dark hair sweeping past her shoulders and hanging in soft waves, even just from bed.

She stopped a short distance from him, taking in where he'd moved the sofa against the wall so he could see who was coming, no blind spots and no way anyone could sneak up on him. His eyes had long since adjusted to the dark, and he noticed the way the shadows lightened from the approaching dawn. The curtains were open, allowing the light in. That way, he could see if anyone was out there.

"You didn't come to bed," she said, then crossed her arms just under the swell of her breasts. "Again."

He didn't move as he took in how distant she sounded: worried, as if they had become two strangers passing in the night. At one time, he'd have been across the room, touching her, being with her, tasting her, loving her—but not now. Not anymore.

It had been so long ago, the last moment he'd been with her. Maybe it was to protect her from him and the darkness that had become a part of who he was. It hadn't killed him yet, but he wished it would. That would destroy her, though.

"Couldn't sleep," he said. "Go back to bed."

He couldn't get up no matter how much he wanted to. And, good for her, she didn't take another step closer. He mourned the necessary loss. He could see the way she hesitated, her lips firmed as if she wanted to say something. Then she must have realized there was no point, as this wasn't a fight she had a chance of winning. He was lost to her. She had to know that.

She turned, and he shut his eyes as she glanced back at him once more from the top of the stairs. "Well, good night, then," she said.

He listened to her footsteps on the stairs, the creak of the wood and the click of the closing door, and let out a breath that sounded far too much like relief, except it was anything but. It did nothing to alieve the burning swell of emptiness that had taken over every good thing in him. It had stolen the part of him that belonged to Annie, because where Sean had gone was a place even the devil didn't go.

CHAPTER 2
SIX MONTHS EARLIER

"This is the last tour, promise, and then we move on," Sean said.

Annie was holding his folded T-shirts as he packed his bags. He wondered for a minute whether this was her way of holding on to him for a little longer. The plain gold band he'd set on her finger two years earlier flashed in the light. Her hand was small, tiny, delicate like the wedding band. It was nothing special, ordinary, but it was all a warrant officer could afford. Unlike the ring, Annie was a diamond, a precious jewel, and she was his.

"You think you'll be happy with the coast guard, just stopping errant tourists?"

Did she have any idea how cute she was? She had no real idea of what he did, and he was happy to keep it that way. She was idealistic, ignorant of the darkness that lurked on the seas.

"It's a little more than that, and plenty to interest me," he said. "I'll be home at night. No more being deployed for months at a time."

The corner of her mouth did a cute little quirk as she tried to hide her smile. He realized it wasn't a real smile, though, because any smile from Annie would light up her entire face even when she tried to hide it. She glanced away, and he reached for her and slid his hand under her chin, tilting her face up so she had to look at him. "I worry about you when I'm gone, and I don't want to, because I'm too far away to do anything for you," he said.

"I know, I'll be okay. Just hurry back. I can't wait to see you, and maybe then we can start our family." She wrapped her arms around his neck, all six hulking feet of him. She was so tiny as she looked up at him, eye level to his chest. She was so short, but she had curves he could really get into. He ran his hand down her back and over her rounded bottom, squeezing.

"Family, huh?" he said. There was a time not long ago that the thought of starting a family had put fear in Annie's eyes and had her backing away, giving all kinds of excuses about why it was a bad idea—mainly that she didn't want to be a single parent, having been raised by one. "What changed your mind?"

The way the light hit her blue eyes, he knew there was something she'd been holding on to. She glanced away, shut her eyes, and then looked back. "I'm tired of being afraid you won't come back. If something does happen, I won't have anything left of you."

The way she was looking at him made him want to clear the bed of his bag and clothes, toss her down, and bury himself deep inside her. But he couldn't. He didn't have time. So he pressed his forehead to hers, brushed his nose with hers. Their lips met, and he kissed her deeply. He could have kept kissing her, looking at her, if she hadn't pulled away and run her tongue over her lower lip, tasting him there.

"You better not start something you can't finish, there, soldier," she said. She could be a flirt when she wanted to be, and she stepped back again. It was then that he noticed she was in her gray tracksuit and cross trainers. Her jacket was unzipped, showing a deep purple top that hugged her curves like a second skin.

"Going for a run?" he said. He didn't really like the fact that she ran alone, without him, even here on base in this part of Florida. She often took a trail used by other servicemen, and he didn't like her being out there alone with them. He'd seen enough of the shady side of some of the enlisted and officers that he didn't want those men anywhere near his wife, and no matter how much she disagreed with him that she was safe, or that she'd be fine, he just didn't want it.

"Just waiting for you to leave, and then I thought I would run a mile or two."

"I'd rather you didn't do it alone, Annie."

She sighed from where she stood at the foot of the bed, resting her hands on her hips. He could tell she was about to argue with him and ignore his warnings to stay safe. "You worry too much, Sean. I'll be fine. It's perfectly safe. It's not as if I'm running at night, and I'm not about to stop running because you're worried about something. Good grief, I could get mugged going into town, at the bank, at the grocery store! Seriously." She turned to pick out a hair tie from the shell she kept on the dresser, then pulled her shoulder-length hair back and slipped the elastic around it.

"And you don't worry enough, Annie. You take chances I don't like."

"You take chances!" she said. "You're gone for how long, and I'm here alone, looking after myself. I don't cross the street without looking both ways, I don't jump out of planes, and I don't walk into bars alone. I'm running to clear my head. It's my time, and I'm not giving it up."

She could be so stubborn. Her gentle nature hid a streak that made her dig in and stand her ground better than any enemy he'd encountered. His wife, whom he loved, had a lot of sides to her that made her anything but ordinary.

He glanced over at the clock and couldn't wait another

moment. He had to go, it wasn't a choice, so he beckoned her toward him—but she stood her ground and even crossed her arms, letting him know she wasn't going to give in. Her face said it all: She was pissed at him.

"Stop fighting me, would you?" he said. He shoved the last of his things into his bag and zipped it up, then reached out and pulled her to him. He could feel how tense she was, how tightly wound, and he gently nudged her as he pulled all her stiffness against him. Of course her stubbornness was something he loved about her, yet here she was fighting the pull between them as she avoided looking at him.

"Hey," he said, sweeping his hand in her hair and pulling it free from the ponytail. "Do you really want me to walk out the door now with us fighting, you being mad at me?"

"Of course not." She rested her hand on his chest and gripped his dark T-shirt.

He kissed her quickly again, then on her cheek, and this time he was the first to let go, but she didn't step away. She stayed beside him as he reached for his bag, and when she looked up again into his eyes, he could see the same confliction that always lay in the shadows. He traced a line down her cheek, and she leaned in, shutting her eyes again as if she needed to memorize his touch.

"I'll call you," he said. "Be good."

She smiled, and this time as he left, he knew she was behind him. She stood there in front of their small house, watching him as he climbed into his pickup and then backed out of the driveway. Sean lifted his hand in a wave as he watched her watching him drive away.

CHAPTER 3

Annie could hear the phone ringing inside the house as she closed the door of her small compact. She hurried as fast as a woman wearing pumps and a pencil skirt could. "I'm coming!" she called out as if whoever was on the phone could hear her.

She shoved the key in the lock and pushed open the door just as the phone stopped ringing, so she placed the paper shopping bag on the bench at the front entryway, tossing her keys and purse down beside it. When she reached for the phone, the screen flashed. There was a message.

She didn't recognize the phone number, but then again, it did say *Private caller*. She hated those blocked numbers. It was probably some telemarketer or salesperson, anyway.

"Seriously, as if I have time for this," she muttered as she dialed the voicemail password and waited. She pulled off her pumps and noticed a run in her pantyhose. Just great—another five bucks down the drain. She was tired after a day of putting out one fire after another at her day job in human resources, and the last thing she wanted was to run back out to the store to buy another pair of nylons. God, she hoped this wasn't a telemarketer or someone else calling to tell her there was a problem. The fact was that she'd been dealing with dickheads all day, busy whining and complaining about everything and anything. The only thing she wanted was to come home, grab a glass of wine, and broil a chicken breast. She didn't want to have to deal with one more challenge of any kind.

She waited for the prompt and then entered her password.

"This message is for Annie Green." It was a deep male voice. "I tried calling you at your office, but you'd already left for the day. I'm a friend of your husband, Sean. If you could give me a call back at this number..." He rattled it off, and she had to fight the clawing fear that something had happened to Sean as she searched for a pen. In the end, she ended up dumping her purse upside down on the floor and found a blue pen and her checkbook. She listened to the message again and scribbled down the phone number across the front of a blank check, all the while fighting panic. All her worries were coming to mind. Had something happened to her husband?

"Oh, God, please don't let anything happen to Sean, please..." She was trembling as she dialed the number, this time pacing the small boxlike living room with a sofa, a chair, and dark occasional tables. All their personal items, pictures and knickknacks she'd spent days boxing up for their move across the country to the Pacific Northwest, were piled off to the side against the wall.

The phone rang once and was answered by the same deep voice that had left the message.

"Hello?" she said. "My name is Annie. You just called about my husband, Sean." She had to clear her throat roughly as she felt her chest tighten. Her head was still running through every scenario of the worst of the worst.

"Annie, thanks for calling right back. I'm a friend of your husband's. My name is Zac."

"Did something happen to Sean? Is he all right?" She

wondered how weak her voice sounded, because to her she sounded so odd. She caught the run in her pantyhose again from the reflection in the hall mirror. Why was it such a big deal? She cradled the phone between her shoulder and ear and reached under her skirt to pull the hose down, hearing a rip as she pulled them off and stepped out of them.

"No, no, Annie. I didn't mean to scare you. Sean is fine, so to speak."

She gripped the wrecked nylons as if she needed them to be able to hear this man. "What do you mean, so to speak? Did something happen? He's coming home next week. We're moving. We're done with the military. We're moving to Seattle. I've already packed up everything." She was rattling on and on.

"Annie, I don't want to alarm you, but I felt it was necessary to call you and let you know that something's happened."

She was staring at herself in the mirror, pale and alone. Sean had been gone so long she couldn't picture him behind her, as she always had done before when she looked in the mirror. "What do you mean, like an accident? When? Where is my husband?" She listened to a sigh on the other end.

"It was weeks ago—"

"Weeks?" she yelled into the phone, cutting the man off. Why in the hell hadn't she been notified? She went over to the small desk and rifled through the letters there, but nothing had been sent to her, and no one had come to the door to notify her that something had happened to Sean. "The navy is supposed to notify me if something happens to my husband."

"Annie, listen to me. Sean wasn't hurt in a way that would require notification. That's why I'm calling."

She was really trying to understand what this man was saying, but he was talking in riddles. She also didn't have a clue who he was. "Who did you say you were again, and which branch of the military are you with?" Maybe this was a hoax and this guy got off on jerking military wives around.

"I'm not with the military, Annie."

"Then I don't understand how you got this number. What is it you want?"

"Sean gave me this number. We've known each other for years. We lost touch for a while, but he called me out of the blue a week ago. He was rattled. Something had happened. All I can say is that I don't know everything, and he can't talk about it, but whatever happened, Sean isn't the same."

She didn't know what to say. This was crazy. "That's ridiculous. What are you saying?"

"I'm saying when Sean came back, he wasn't the same, and when you see him, he won't be the same. Sometimes men walk into things in a war that mess them up forever."

"You're wrong. I know Sean. He's strong, and he never lets anything rattle him. When he gets back stateside, he'll prove—"

"He's already back. That's what I'm trying to tell you," Zac said. She could hear him talking to someone in the background then, and there was a rustle as if he was passing the phone over.

"Annie," Sean said in a voice that sounded so strange, so tired. But it was him.

"Sean, where are you? What's going on?"

"Hey, baby, listen. Have you packed up everything?"

"Yes, movers are coming next week. Where are you? Oh my God, why didn't you tell me you were back? When did you leave? Why didn't you call me?" Her mind was racing, and she wanted to hammer him with questions, demand answers, the first being *Why aren't you here now with me?*

He didn't say anything for a moment. There was just dead air, and she wondered whether he was still there.

"Sean, Sean, are you still there?"

"Yeah, listen, um…" He cleared his throat, and the only

thing that accomplished was to make her panic rise again. Where was her take-charge husband, the man who took care of everything, including her?

"Sean, talk to me. You're scaring me."

"I'm sorry, Annie. I don't mean to scare you. I'm getting our house ready here in Port Angeles. It'll be fine."

She didn't understand any of this. It was as if she'd just stepped into a B movie. "No, Seattle, remember? We're moving to Seattle." What the hell was going on with him?

"Change of plans, Annie. A position came up here in Port Angeles with the coast guard, and I jumped at it. I already cancelled the lease for the house in Seattle and got us a sweet place here. You'll love it."

Oh no, this was not happening after all the hoops she'd had to jump through to get a position in Seattle with their sister office. It was a step down in the human resources department, but still a good job. "You can't do that," she said. "I have a job already lined up in Seattle. Port Angeles, what the hell am I going to do there? No, Sean, you talk to me. You don't make decisions on the fly without talking to me first. This is a marriage. We talk, you listen to me, we discuss, we make plans." She was breathing hard, so furious she was spitting. She wanted to pull him through the phone line. This wasn't Sean. He'd never decided anything of this magnitude without talking with her. Even when he made decisions, she was always in the loop. Right now, she felt as if she'd been banished to the back forty.

She could hear him breathing on the other end. What the hell was he thinking? He sure in the hell hadn't talked to her or even let her know he was back. No, this couldn't be happening. Now they were moving to some place she'd never even been. She pressed her hand to her throat. "The movers are scheduled for Thursday—this Thursday, Sean," she said. "In five days, they'll be taking our things to Seattle."

"Call them. Change it."

Was he serious? She pulled the phone away and stared at it, wondering who she was talking to. There was a rustle in the background again.

"Annie, it's Zac."

"Zac," she said. He was a stranger, but right now it seemed he was her only link to sanity. "Zac, are you telling me Sean expects us, me, to move to Port Angeles and just change plans, just like that?"

"Yeah, um, I'm not really sure about everything that's going on, Annie, but I've got Sean here and we'll sort it out. Do you need help making arrangements?"

Was he serious? What was this man going to do? She lifted her hand in the air, at a loss. As she took in the ruined nylons in her hand, she realized this wasn't sane. "So I'm doing this alone? Sean isn't coming home to help with the move," she said, more for effect. She already understood from this fucked-up conversation that she had been tossed to the wolves.

"What do you need to do still?" Zac asked.

Now she couldn't help feeling bad. This wasn't on Zac, yet even she could hear the bitchiness in her voice. It should have been Sean getting the full effect from her, but Zac was a stranger, and she'd been raised better than that.

"Tomorrow is my last day at work, but Sean's truck is still here, and my car… Then we were supposed to stop at his parents' on the drive across the country. Has he even called his parents?"

"Sean hasn't talked to anyone, Annie, just you now. Annie, listen, give me the name of the movers you hired. I'll call them, get your car towed and make arrangements for Sean's truck. You get a ticket to fly up here. I'll get Sean to call his parents and let them know about the change of plans. He can do that much."

"I was planning on driving. Both Sean and I were." *Change of plans* was an understatement, but she realized that not driving across the country from Florida would be easier. "You're right," she said. "I'll fly." She rifled through the desk for the movers' card and read the number off to Zac.

"Finish packing, and call me back when you know your flight," he said.

She should have been talking to Sean, her husband, not a stranger. As she hung up, she realized that her husband's friend, a man she didn't know, was suddenly doing what Sean had always done. She found it extremely unsettling.

CHAPTER 4

Moving to a new house could be exciting, but moving across the country to a house she had never seen, to a husband she didn't know, had left Annie scrambling to find her footing.

She heard the front door click closed and men chatting, then noticed Sean and his friend Zac come in. Zac was a former marine: tall, handsome, with dark hair, a badass attitude, and a scarred face. Annie was still dumbfounded by the change in Sean, though. On the outside, he was the same tall, dark, and handsome man she'd married, but he was far from solid and dependable now. He'd changed, and if anyone asked, she wouldn't be able to tell them exactly why.

"Sounds like a plan," Sean said to Zac, clearly unaware Annie was standing behind a box in the corner of the kitchen. But Zac's gaze was astute and went right to her. He jutted his chin toward her, and maybe that was what alerted Sean. That was so unusual, because he and Annie had always been so in tune with each other, knowing where the other was as soon as they entered a room. It was their energy, a chemistry between them that she could have sworn, a short time ago, would never disappear.

"Annie," Sean said, but he made no move to close the distance between them. It was the same as when she'd arrived three days before. He had yet to touch her in any way, hug her, hold her, or kiss her. He treated her like a roommate, and now he was holding himself back, away from her, as if they were merely sharing space.

Zac was watching Sean closely. "My wife, Diane—you haven't had a chance to meet her yet, but she's hoping you'll come by for dinner," he said as he turned to Annie, who was standing there, holding an open box of glasses. "Here, let me take that." He placed the box on the counter, which was piled with kitchenware, plastic, and utensils.

Sean hadn't moved. In fact, he was watching her and then Zac, fisting his hands. His face didn't show an ounce of emotion, and that was starting to freak her out. She wanted to run her hand over his arm and then slip it around his waist, and she wanted him to pull her close and kiss the top of her head. But she couldn't make her feet move, because she knew he wouldn't let her get close to him, so she linked her hands together when she realized Zac was watching her.

"Ah, sounds great," she said, though it wasn't. She was being polite, but she had no desire to make polite conversation with some stranger when she wanted nothing more than to spend some time alone with Sean and try to get to the bottom of what was going on with him. "When?"

"Tonight." He checked his watch and then patted Sean's shoulder as he started past.

Sean, though, was rubbing the back of his neck as if he had other ideas. Annie wondered again, as she had every minute since she'd arrived, whether Sean was about to drop a bomb on her and tell her he was shipping out, moving, or selling everything out from under her—basically kicking her to the curb. As bizarre as it was, she couldn't shake the feeling that Sean was doing everything he could not to be with her.

"Why don't you take Annie with you now?" he said. "I'll

catch up." Then he actually walked away, leaving Annie watching him round the corner to the stairwell and up the stairs to their bedroom, where he shut the door.

She could feel her jaw slacken as she watched helplessly. Four months ago, she would have sworn that hell would freeze over before Sean would let another man take her anywhere.

Zac was shaking his head. "How are you doing, Annie?"

"Are you kidding me? What's going on with my husband?" She gestured to the stairs, toward the bedroom he'd yet to sleep in with her. It had been three days since she'd stepped off a small plane in Port Angeles to see Sean standing there with Zac, three days since she'd stepped up to do the one thing she and Sean had never had any trouble doing: hugging, holding, kissing. Instead, he'd stepped to the side and gestured to Zac, behaving more like a mere acquaintance than the loving husband she adored.

Zac let nothing show on his face. Instead, he reached for the sunglasses tucked in his dark brown shirtfront and lifted them out as if he was getting ready to put them back on. Then he lowered his hand and took a step toward her, closer until he was right in front of her. "He's dealing with some issues, some things he can't talk to you about. Only he can work through them." He didn't take his eyes off her as he spoke. She wanted to ask about the scar on his face, but it was becoming less distracting the more she knew him.

"I'm his wife, Zac. He should tell me, talk to me. He shouldn't be keeping secrets."

Zac gave her an odd look and shook his head gently, stepping closer still. "You're wrong, Annie. Sean has been in the military for a lot of years. Has he come home and talked to you about what he's seen, what he's done?"

She was about to deny it, to say that of course they shared things—but she knew better. Sean had never talked about what he did, had never given any detail. She realized Zac's question had been hypothetical. She swallowed as she took him in, and then it struck her: His dangerous looks should have made her nervous, but instead he was striking, attractive. There was something solid about Zac that had once been a part of her husband, something she missed desperately.

"I want to know what's going on with him. He won't touch me, Zac, or sleep in the same bed as me. He avoids me. We've become strangers. My husband is now a stranger to me!" she shouted. "I don't know what to do. I feel as if my world is spinning out of control. I don't know how to reach him." Her voice cracked this time as she fought to keep it down.

"You may not be able to reach him," Zac said. "He'll never be the same. There are things in life that change all of us. We're always evolving, changing, but some things don't shape us for the good. Sometimes we find ourselves in a darkness we don't know how to get out of, and that's where Sean is. He's drowning in it, and he's not going to allow you to get dragged into it."

She didn't really understand what Zac was saying, but she had a pretty good idea that whatever had happened to Sean, she might never get him back. Three days ago, she hadn't believed it, but being around Sean and seeing the way he was now…

"I don't even have a job," she said. "I moved here for Sean, and I don't know whether he's going to be here tomorrow or the next day. What am I going to do? I don't know anyone here. Sean's family is on the other side of the country. Mine, too." She lowered herself and perched on the edge of one of the boxes, taking in the open kitchen with light wood that was so plain and ordinary and not hers. "I don't mean to complain. I just don't know how to reach him. How long am I supposed to sit on the sidelines like this and pretend that any of this is okay?"

Zac started to say something and then stopped. "Come for dinner tonight, meet my wife. We'll help you get this figured out and find you a job. It'll be all right." Zac was so kind and together. She really wished he could straighten out her husband.

"Will it, Zac, really?"

He didn't answer her. He didn't even try to lie to her.

She didn't know what made her look up, but when she did, she saw Sean standing in the doorway of the kitchen, watching Zac watching her. It wasn't so much that she didn't know how long he'd been standing there. What bothered her was the look in his eyes, which was anything but friendly.

CHAPTER 5

She was the most beautiful woman he'd ever laid eyes on, and she was giving all her attention to Zac, talking to him as if he were her confidant. By the way she flushed and glanced down, he knew he'd caught her talking about him behind his back.

"Sean, I didn't hear you come down," she said, glancing to Zac, who was standing rather close to her—too close for Sean's liking.

Zac made no move to step away from Annie. As he turned and faced him, his expression gave nothing away.

"What the fuck, Zac?" Sean said. "Are you moving in on my wife?"

"Don't be an asshole," Zac replied. This time, he stepped away from Annie, tucking the sunglasses in his hand back into his shirtfront and then stepping toward Sean as if he was going to kick his ass.

Sean didn't miss Annie's look of hurt. It seemed that was all he could manage to do as of late.

"Really, Sean?" She sounded choked. She, of anyone… He would rather slit his wrists than hurt her.

"I step out of the room for a second and come back in to

you two talking about me. Seriously, Zac? She's my wife. Are you trying to turn her against me?"

"Look at you," Zac said. "Fuck, man, you're so paranoid. Pull your head out of your ass, Sean. Annie can't talk to you because of you pushing her away, and you refuse to talk to her. Hell, you dragged her across the country and made her handle everything because you came back so totally fucked up. She's supposed to drop everything for you?"

Sean was squeezing his hands into fists and breathing hard. He could see Annie standing there as if she was afraid to move. Zac, a friend he'd known for years, was standing in front of her as if protecting her. He didn't like it one bit. Even though Zac had left the military years before, he had always been someone Sean knew would have his back.

"It's fine, Zac," Annie started to say, but Zac was shaking his head, never taking his eyes off Sean. He didn't turn toward Annie, and he didn't move from where he stood in Sean's space, right in front of him, so close that Sean could take a swing at him. He could take him down, too. He was sure he could.

"No, it's not," Zac said. "Sean, your wife had to quit her job. She had one lined up where you were supposed to move in Seattle, but now here she is"—he gestured toward the ceiling—"in this godforsaken place because you couldn't even tell her the real reason you're here or why you left that position at the coast guard base in Seattle. Here in Port Angeles, there's less pay, less everything. Come on, Sean. Let's get real."

The last thing Sean wanted was for Annie to hear about how he'd been forced to retire from the military, about his medical discharge, about the fact that his job in Seattle had been taken off the table by his superiors—all because one night had left two of his team members dead. All because Sean had screwed up. It was something he was going to have to live with, something he was going to have to bear, but his wife wasn't going to ever hear one detail of it. Now he regretted everything he had shared with Zac.

"You say one word…"

"And you'll what? Grow up, Sean. We all screw up. You don't hold the corner on that, so be a man about it and move on. Right now, you're behaving worse than a teenager. Your wife deserves better. Talk to her, for fuck's sake." Zac was spitting mad, and Sean wasn't happy at having his shortcomings pointed out to him.

"What is Zac talking about, Sean?" Annie said. "What happened? What is this all about? Why did we move here?" He didn't have to look over at her to know she was stepping closer, up to Zac's side. "Sean…"

He couldn't tell her. He wouldn't tell her. He just stared at Zac, who stared back at him as if either of them had to break first. "You're a stubborn asshole," Sean said. "Would you want Diane knowing, if this was you? Would you tell her? Have you told her about everything you've seen, done?"

At times, Zac's expression could go stone cold as if he didn't feel a thing. "She's my wife. I tell her what I tell her, and that ain't no concern of yours. Right now, yours doesn't know what the hell is up with you or whether she's going to wake up tomorrow to find that you've hightailed it out of here."

Sean wanted to deny it, as if nothing like that would happen, but the fact was that Zac was right. He was barely holding anything together. Every minute of every hour over the past few days, he had wrestled with the fact that Annie might be better off without him. "Fuck you!" he said, shoving Zac before starting toward the door.

"Sean!" Annie yelled behind him. "Where are you going?"

He paused for just a second in the open door, but he didn't turn around. She put her hand on his arm, and his gaze went right to it. He could feel the instant his muscle tightened even though he didn't want her touching him, but his body had other ideas, so he just stared at her hand until she slowly pulled it away.

"Out," he said. "I need some air." Then he stepped outside their ordinary two-story house on their quiet street in their quiet neighborhood, the type of place only good people lived. Now, that was the one thing Sean wasn't.

CHAPTER 6

"I don't understand why you just can't tell me," Annie said. She was buckled into the passenger side of Zac's pickup. It was one of those newer models with dark blue cloth seats and a lot of features, a style that seemed to fit him. He was an interesting man, quiet at times, deep and brooding, a man whose demeanor could fool someone into thinking he was one of those nice guys who kept to himself, minded his own business, and did his own thing.

That was true to a point, except he was hiding a part of himself. Even she could see it. He took in everything the minute he saw it, touched it, smelled it. It was so subtle, not something she had noticed right away. It was something she had only recently realized from being around him. He was a man who could lurk in the shadows like a panther, ready to pounce, biding his time, cold and calculating and protective, too. She should have been scared of a man like Zac, but she found him oddly comforting. At the same time, she was envious of Diane, his wife, a woman she was about to meet. She wondered what kind of woman had captured the attention of a man like him.

He never took his eyes off the road, and not only did he

not answer her right away, he seemed to be pulled away in his own thoughts. "The promise that I wouldn't tell is going to have to be good enough, Annie. Sean is my friend. This is something he has to tell you himself, and no amount of poking and prodding on your part is going to make him open up until he's ready. I just won't tell you." He glanced over her way, and she was clear now on one more thing about Zac. He had a way of throwing her off. Just when she thought he was in his head, somewhere else, he was suddenly back and hadn't missed a thing. All of a sudden, she had all of his attention.

"I may have pushed too hard earlier," he said. "I was angry and lost my cool. Give Sean time. He has to work through this himself just like every other soldier. Some have been through worse, others not, but everyone handles things differently. Let me be clear: Sean may very well be keeping himself away from you to protect you from him, so you need to respect that much about him."

That made no sense at all. She'd always been able to talk to Sean, always.

"So how'd you two meet?" Zac asked.

For a minute, she wondered who he was talking about. "Oh, you mean me and Sean."

He glanced back to the road as a hint of a smile touched his lips.

"Grocery store, of all places. While I was bagging up oranges, he asked me how to tell if a melon was ripe. For one minute, I didn't think he was serious. I knew right away he was hitting on me, so I picked a ripe one, handed it to him, and walked away, but he just wouldn't let me walk off. He dogged my heels, even followed me to the cashier and paid for his melon, hurrying out of the store after me. I just couldn't get past his smile, his persistence."

"Sounds like stalking," Zac said.

"It probably was, but he asked me out for coffee, so I

walked with him to a corner stand, and we talked for two hours. The rest is history, really. I gave him my number, he moved me in a few weeks later, and he shipped out the following month."

"And you waited for him while he was gone."

She couldn't help the wistful smile that touched her lips as she thought back to the days when he returned, the hours they'd spent making love, touching, and the moment he hurried her to a justice of the peace and slid his ring on her finger. From that moment, she'd belonged to Sean. "Of course."

"Hmm" was all Zac said.

"Why would you ask that? Of course I waited. Why wouldn't I?"

"It takes a special woman to wait around for a man in the military, to marry a man who'll spend more time away than home with his wife. All that time away is like a wedge that drives between a relationship until the two can no longer find their way back to each other."

What an odd thing for Zac to say. She really wondered about his story, about how he'd gotten those burns on the side of his face and what kind of past he shared with Sean. "Tell me about you, Zac. How long have you and Diane been married?"

"Not long, almost a year." He flicked the right signal light.

She listened to it tick while he turned down a gravel road. They were in the country, with a few houses scattered here and there, but the land was dense, with plenty of trees that were becoming heavier. "Newlyweds still. How did you meet?"

He was worse than Sean, or maybe the same, not really forthcoming about himself. "Over a murder. She was the investigating detective. I was working with the coroner's office." He didn't look her way, and she was surprised, because she hadn't realized his wife was a cop. Somehow, she hadn't pictured Zac being with a woman with such a demanding career. Why had she thought his relationship would be something safe, too? That would be ridiculous, since men like Sean and Zac weren't really safe at all, were they?

"You don't talk much about yourself, Zac. I'm feeling a little insecure, here. You know a lot about me, probably far more than I'm comfortable with. You, on the other hand, I know nothing about. Until you phoned, I didn't even know you were a friend of my husband's." She also knew that Sean had many friends in the military, probably more than she knew about, but she found it odd that out of everyone, even his family—although they weren't close—Sean had chosen to reach out to Zac. So what exactly was it between them that made them know each other well enough that in times of trouble, Zac was Sean's go-to? "How do you know Sean?"

He darted a glance to Annie, but she didn't have a clue what he was thinking. His expression was blank as if he could hide anything.

"I mean how could you have met other than in the military?" she said. "More to the point, my husband sought you out and pulled this disappearing/reappearing change of plans, and the only person he consulted was you, not me."

He darted another glance her way.

"You're not answering, which really makes me wonder what's between you and my husband. It makes me feel like the odd man out."

"Whatever you're thinking, Annie, it's not that."

"Well, what is it, then? Enlighten me."

She could tell she'd hit a nerve, as his face tightened. His lips thinned, and he let out a breath as he pulled into a private treed driveway leading to a lovely white A-frame. It had green trim, a welcoming front porch with a glassed-in overhang, and a small pond with a waterfall garden in front.

It was tranquil, peaceful, and so not the picture of the man beside her.

The front door opened, and a woman of medium height and build with short cropped hair and deep brown eyes stepped out.

"He saved my life," Zac said. "I owe him everything, and that's an unbreakable bond."

She turned and stared at the man beside her as he climbed out of the truck, stepped up on the porch, and kissed the woman, who was the furthest thing from the image Annie had conjured up of the type of woman who would be with Zac. It just went to show her that appearances could be more than deceiving.

CHAPTER 7

Sean didn't know how long he had been sitting on the log, tossing rocks into the ocean, but he'd cooled off enough that he felt the cold reality of what an ass he'd been—going off on Zac like that as if the man would move in on his wife. That was something that couldn't happen, wouldn't happen. He shut his eyes and tried to let it go. "Jesus, Sean, pull it together," he said. He just couldn't help the feeling that maybe he was burning his bridges faster than he had any hope of repairing them.

He could also tell, as the late afternoon sun dipped lower in the sky, that it was getting late. He heard the ding on his cell phone again as another message popped up from Zac: *Where are you?* He thumbed through the other five, all from Zac. He'd talked Annie into coming for dinner, he was driving her over, and Sean should still come. He should at least stop in and apologize. He should at least pick up his wife and take her home. But he made no move to get up.

He glanced down the rocky beach to a young family, a father and his son holding his mother's hand. What he'd give for that to be his life, easy and carefree, without one worry. A simple life was all he wanted, but right now it seemed so out of reach. The life he'd come from while growing up had seemed boring, but now he wished he could go back to that. He should call his parents. After the hurried message he'd left that he and Annie wouldn't be stopping by, they'd called back, worried, wondering what was going on, and he'd yet to return their call—to tell them what any good son would: where he was, where he was going, and that everything was all right.

His cell phone rang, and instead of ignoring it, he answered on the first ring.

"Sean, it's Zac. Dinner's ready. We're just about to eat. Wanted to know if you're coming."

He didn't know what to say. Of course he should go. He wanted to. "I don't know if that's such a good idea," he replied. He could hear talking in the background: Diane, he assumed, and Annie. Then there was quiet.

"Of course it is. We'll wait for you. Where are you?"

Would Zac come looking for him? "Just sitting by the ocean, some pullout."

"Well, get your ass over here. Get in your truck. We'll wait." Zac didn't say anything else, but Sean could hear him breathing on the other end.

"No, man, I'm not fit company. I shouldn't be there."

"Hey, you don't need to be perfect. What you do need is to be here. Come on."

What was it about Zac that made him seem like the only voice of reason that could cut through all the bullshit of life, all the memories that were yanking at his sanity like fishing hooks? It was Zac who seemed to be able to pull out each hook one by one in a way that could, for a second, help Sean breathe.

"Fine, but you've been warned," he said.

"See you soon."

Sean stood up, shoving his hands in his jean pockets, feeling the chill through his dark hoodie. With a last look at the family before climbing up the rocky bank, he started back to his truck.

He made the drive to Zac's in less than fifteen minutes, and the closer he got, he felt his hands sweating and the dampness beading up his back. Why the hell was he so nervous? What was wrong with him? He pulled up behind Zac's pickup, which was parked beside Diane's four-door SUV, then sat there, just staring at the picture-perfect house and the life that Zac had built for himself. He'd never expected this of Zac. Of anyone he'd served with, Zac had been so fucked up from the loss of his lady and the baby she carried that Sean hadn't thought he'd ever trust a woman again. But Zac had proved him wrong.

Sean liked Diane, maybe because she wasn't the typical woman Zac went after. She seemed to carry the same dark, brooding demeanor. She was a woman with secrets, maybe a troubled past. He could only guess.

The front door opened, and Zac stood there, watching him. He didn't say anything as Sean climbed out of his truck and started toward him, his feet crunching the gravel. Sound carried out here, more distinct, louder, much more than in the city, which was so noisy that everything blended into a buzz. He stopped at the foot of the steps and looked up at Zac.

"You're late," Zac said, then stepped outside, opening up the doorway as if all was clear.

"Well I came, didn't I?"

Zac gave a hint of a smile as he glanced away and then back to Sean. "You did. It's a start." He gestured toward the kitchen with his thumb. "Let's eat."

CHAPTER 8

The dining room had soft green walls with crown molding painted a crisp shade of white. Two windows filled one wall, bringing light into the room that didn't allow for shadows to linger in the corners. Diane was sitting across the round table from Annie, with an empty chair between them. The table was laid out with cheeses, crackers, marinated artichokes, and an appetizer that Zac had placed in between them. Annie was grateful, at least, as it kept her from toppling over drunk from one glass of wine. Diane was drinking some fruity drink. Annie wasn't sure exactly what it was, but it was alcohol free, something she would have preferred. Zac had insisted she have some wine, though. Maybe he thought she needed loosening up.

"Again, really, thanks for having me for dinner," she said. She was nervous even though Diane had made every attempt to put her at ease.

"Look who's finally dragged his sorry ass in here," Zac said from the entryway. Sean stepped into the dining room with him, still wearing a dark hoodie and blue jeans that hung low on his hips. He glanced at Annie before directing his gaze to Diane, whom he offered a smile.

"Diane, thanks for the invite," he said, standing off to the side.

Annie couldn't help feeling an uneasy jealousy sweep over her. It was unwelcome.

"Good to see you," Diane said. "Besides, Zac's cooking. I'm just sitting here while he does all the work."

Zac handed Sean a beer and gestured to Annie's empty glass. She started to shake her head, but he took the glass from her anyway. "You're not driving," he said before returning a second later with another full glass.

Good grief, had the tension in the room just soared? Even Diane sensed something, with the way she was looking between Sean and Annie. Then she extended the flat of her hand to the chair on Annie's right. "Sit down, Sean," she said. "I believe Zac is bringing in the…what did you make, Zac?"

Whatever he was making smelled amazing—the spices, the aroma. Diane was one lucky woman, having a husband who looked like Zac cooking for her.

"Curry chicken," he said. "Didn't ask you, Annie, if you're okay with a little spice or if there's anything you don't like."

"She's fine," Sean said, cutting in before Annie could answer for herself. Then he reached for the chair beside her, pulled it out, and sat down.

Zac gave Sean an odd look before directing his gaze to Annie again. "Annie?" he asked, making it clear he wanted nothing to do with the crap Sean was dishing out.

"I'm not a picky eater," she said. "Whatever you've made, by the smells coming from the kitchen, I'm sure it'll be great." She glanced to Sean, who was leaning forward, his arms resting on the table as he glanced over his shoulder to her. It was so subtle, but he was wound tight, holding himself away from her. She was pretty sure that if she reached out and touched him, he'd be out of the chair and gone. It was disturbing.

So she smiled, reached for her glass of wine, and took a healthy swallow.

"So, Annie, tell me, how's the house?" Diane said. Annie had been watching her, and there was something about her. She was far from a beauty queen, but at the same time, she was real. So genuine. Annie really liked her.

"Well, I'm still looking for everything in the boxes. It'll take some time, but hopefully the next few days I can get everything unpacked and organized, put away. Then I need to find a job, since I wasn't expecting to be living here." She stopped herself from adding that she'd basically burned bridges with her employer after all the strings they'd pulled to get her lined up with a job in Seattle, basically holding it for her, which had inconvenienced a hell of a lot of people. It was a call she hadn't liked making, letting them know that oops, by the way, so sorry, but her husband had just returned and decided on a whim that they weren't moving to Seattle but instead relocating to Port Angeles. It wasn't sane, and she was still mortified at having to go in and explain.

"Fuck," Sean muttered. He was shaking his head beside her as if she was carrying on like a spoiled child.

Diane, however, was looking from her to Sean again. Then she glanced up as Zac set down two steaming bowls of rice and a curry chicken with cream sauce. It looked amazing.

"Yeah, Annie is looking for a job," Zac said as he pulled out a chair beside Diane, across from Sean, and sat down. There was an open beer already in front of his plate. "Was going to mention it to you, if you can keep your ear to the ground."

"You don't need a job," Sean added, still leaning forward. He lifted his beer and took a swallow. Maybe he was trying to make sure everyone had heard him the first time, even though she was sure they were ignoring him. Sean wasn't looking at her but straight ahead at no one in particular. Was he serious? She knew her mouth was agape as she looked to

Zac and then over to Diane, whose face didn't give anything away.

"What exactly are you looking for?" Diane asked Annie as if she hadn't heard Sean. Maybe she was used to dealing with idiotic alphas who didn't have their heads screwed on right.

"Well, administrative. HR is my specialty. I've worked as an HR assistant for the past two years, but I don't think there's a big demand for corporate HR types way out here."

"There's always something for someone," Diane said. "I'll keep my ear open and will let you know if I hear of something, but you may want to get some resumes out."

No one said anything else as the food was passed around and dished up. Annie listened as Sean and Zac talked about nothing and everything, from the current state of the military, to the coast guard station, to Zac's project building a sunroom off the back of the house, which she hadn't even noticed. She looked to Diane, who shrugged. "He's not happy unless he's doing something," she said.

"Hey, not true!" Zac slipped his arm around Diane, pulling her closer so she was tucked up against him. She looked up at him and smiled, and he leaned in and kissed her before pulling away and scooting back his chair. He started to clear the dishes from the table.

"See?" Diane added as Sean joined Zac and took the leftover food into the kitchen. The men were still talking, but in the other room now.

"*Wow* is all I can say. He cooks, builds, and cleans up?" Annie said as Diane leaned back, crossing her arms over her plain peach shirt just as Zac walked back in with a washcloth and wiped the table down.

"Some of the things that attracted me to him," Diane said. Zac kissed her again as she ran her hand up his arm. "One of the first things he ever did for me was cook."

Annie would've never figured Diane as a touchy-feely woman, but the chemistry between her and Zac was so connected, a bond that she'd thought, at one time, she had with Sean.

Zac leaned down again, so close he could have kissed Diane, as a hint of a smile touched his lips. "That was, of course, after you shot me."

"You shot him?" Annie couldn't keep the shock from her voice, but Diane made a face as if he was whining.

"Grazed you, was all. He bled all over my kitchen, then cleaned and stitched himself up, too." Diane was suddenly pale—not so much a tough girl, after all.

Maybe Zac had realized how bothered she pretended not to be, as he slid his finger under her chin and tilted it up. "I'm okay."

Something passed between them then, a lot of secrets, forcing Annie to swallow hard with longing. She glanced up at Sean. who was watching her with something she couldn't put into words.

"Zac. why don't you show me what you've done since I was here last," he said. He looked uncomfortable and had immediately crushed the moment between Diane and Zac. "How about another beer, too? he added. Zac, who was already nodding, stepped away from Diane. His hand lingered on hers briefly before falling away. "Diane?" Sean said to her, but she shook her head and then flushed.

"No, this girl's off all alcohol," she said, looking at Zac. Maybe Sean hadn't picked up on it, but Annie had.

"Are you pregnant?"

Diane appeared uncomfortable and fidgeted for a minute. "Yeah, we just found out."

"Congratulations, dude!" Sean slapped Zac's shoulder the way guys do and then slung his arm around it for a second, grinning over at Diane. "Didn't know that was something you two were planning."

Zac's expression softened as he stared over at Diane. "Was just waiting for Diane to be ready. Took long enough."

Annie figured that was a private joke between them.

"So does that mean you're retiring your badge?" Sean asked Diane, and Annie wondered the same, realizing they hadn't talked much about Diane being a cop.

"Yes," Zac said at the same time Diane said, "No."

Zac appeared to darken, filling the room with male energy as if he had every right to tell her what to do. "You are turning in your badge," he said. "We've discussed this. I'm not going to be worrying about you every day walking out of this house with my kid in you and something happening to you, to both of you." He didn't yell, but this was a side of Zac Annie hadn't seen before, going all alpha. Diane didn't seem affected at all.

In fact, she actually laughed at him and shook her head. "No, I'm not. You may think you can tell me what to do, but this is my career, and I fought my way to this position, having to deal with all those tough-ass pricks who saw me as weak—"

"You are done with OPNET, and I don't give a shit what all those asshole cops think about you. You'll turn in your badge and tell them you're pregnant. We talked about this. You know how I feel."

"I'm not going to give those cops any more reason to see me as weak."

Annie couldn't believe how unbending Diane was being with Zac. In fact, Annie was a little nervous about Zac's overbearing reaction, and Sean just stood there, watching the two of them in the background.

"Weak? Shit." Zac gestured in the air as he turned to Sean, who appeared to be giving Zac all his support.

"Yes, weak," Diane said. "You heard me. I already told you I wouldn't put the baby at risk, but I'm not quitting. Besides, my sergeant will park me on a desk as soon as he finds out."

That didn't seem to appease Zac in the least as he stepped

closer to Diane, crossed his arms, and stared down at her. "Until something happens, as it always does, and you're called out into the field. I know you, Diane. You'll go without thinking twice about it." He was shaking his head again, his lips stretched to a fine line. "No." He swiped his hand to the side as if this was off the table, discussion finished.

"I'm not Lizzy" was all Diane said, so softly that Zac went quiet. He just watched her, saying nothing.

When Annie looked over at Sean, he was shaking his head with a look of sadness. It seemed everyone knew who Lizzy was except her.

CHAPTER 9

Annie couldn't remember the last time she'd sat beside Sean in his truck as he drove them home. "Who's Lizzy?" she finally asked. Whatever it was about Lizzy had pretty much put a damper on the evening, and Sean had made their excuses and ushered Annie out of Zac and Diane's.

Sean was rubbing his hand over his jaw, and she could hear the rustle of a few days' stubble. On Sean it didn't look messy. It was just another thing about him that he could pull off, making him look damn sexy but still untouchable. She could tell he was thinking, maybe about whether to answer her or not.

"Zac's girlfriend. She was pregnant with his child." That was all he said as he sat there, driving them home to their new house, which felt strange and far from being theirs.

"So Zac has another child?" Annie said. There had been no mention of kids. For that matter, she hadn't seen any photos of children around, the kind that parents always had hanging on their walls to show proudly to everyone who stopped in.

This time, Sean did glance her way, but he was shaking his head. "No, he has no kids. His baby died."

What the hell could she say to that? She couldn't imagine losing a child. Maybe that was why Zac was the way he was.

"Lizzy was Zac's downfall," Sean added as he drove, running his finger over his lip, evidently thinking some pretty dark thoughts. "She killed their baby."

He pulled into their driveway and parked behind her compact, shoving the truck in park before turning the engine off. All Annie could do was sit there, shocked at hearing something so horrible. How could a woman kill her baby? It was a picture in her head that she didn't want.

"Was she mentally ill?" she asked. That was the only explanation for something so dark and twisted.

Sean opened his door to get out and then stopped and glanced at her. "Was who mentally ill?" he asked before climbing out before she could finish. He was coming around the front of the truck, but Annie opened her door and stepped out.

"Lizzy, the woman you just said killed her baby. I mean, is she in jail?"

He gave her a confused look and then shook his head as he started toward the house, keys jingling in his hands. He shoved the key in the lock and turned it, then took a breath before glancing over at Annie. He was so close to her, and she realized this was the first time he hadn't stepped back and moved out of her space since she'd stepped off that plane three days before.

"Lizzy was a midwife working with Doctors without Borders. Zac met her in Afghanistan, where he was stationed. She was beautiful and arrogant, confident, not someone a man could control, definitely not the type to settle down. But Zac had other ideas, thinking he could soften her. She got pregnant over there and stayed. She was supposed to ship out before the baby was born, and I don't know how she was still there. I don't think Zac did, either. She was in high demand there, and arrangements had been made for her to go back to Denmark before the baby was born. Zac had arranged leave to be at the birth of his child."

Sean was shaking his head and pulled his hand away from the closed door. He faced Annie, looking down at her. "She didn't tell Zac she hadn't left. All we know is a call came in that she had gone to Syria, to some camp with a group of doctors. They were needed. Instead of looking after the baby and going home, she didn't hesitate to put herself at risk and go with those doctors. Guess she figured she was invincible, and if it was just her, it would have been her choice. They never made it to the camp."

Annie shut her eyes at the horror. No wonder Zac wanted Diane to quit. She couldn't blame him. "So Lizzy was killed on the way."

Sean was so tall. He gazed over her head to the outside light that was on behind her. "We were in camp. I was there with Zac when he found out what she had done. I don't even remember how he found out, but I've never seen Zac lose it like that. He went AWOL as soon as he found that Lizzy had gone into Syria. He went after her in one of the Humvees. It took Zac a long time to tell me what happened when he found her." Sean was shaking his head, and for a minute she was sure there were tears in his eyes.

"He came upon their transport in flames and heard the screams. Lizzy was already dead. He dragged her dead body out and cut the baby out of her. Maya, his baby girl—he tried to save her, but it was too late. He wrapped up that dead baby and set her tiny body in his Humvee. He was going to bring her back, he said later, when the vehicle was hit. We found him barely alive, and there was nothing left." Sean stopped. There were tears in his eyes, and he swiped at them and sniffed, stepping back as if he had just remembered he needed to put distance between them. "His burns, months of skin grafts…" He cleared his throat again and shook his head. "Our colonel pulled strings so Zac wasn't thrown in the brig. He was given a dishonorable discharge, though. Can you blame him for hating Lizzy?"

Sean opened the door and walked into the house. All Annie could do was stand there, watching him, reeling from a story that had left her shell shocked.

CHAPTER 10

He'd never meant to share Zac's story with Annie. He didn't know why he'd chosen that moment to share a memory that had ripped Zac's world apart. He poured himself a glass of water, feeling sick at even talking about what had happened. It had gutted Zac, finding Lizzy cut up and having to pull the baby from her. Her eyes had been lifeless, staring straight up at nothing. Although Zac hated her with every ounce of his being, Sean couldn't help mourning her loss.

He could feel Annie before she said anything, standing behind him, her long dark hair hanging in waves past her shoulders. Her face was sad and gorgeous, and she looked at him as if she was so alone. He hadn't even noticed what she wore: It was just a simple brown T-shirt and a pair of blue jeans, but it made her look irresistible.

"Why didn't you ever tell me?" she said. She gestured helplessly, and it was then that he realized she had no clue about the things he'd seen, the things he'd done. Even though he hated the lost look on her face now, the look he'd put there after turning her life upside down, he knew with certainty that if she ever learned the horrible things he was capable of, she'd see him as a monster, and that was something he knew he couldn't bear.

"That isn't something you needed in your head," he said. "Hell, I wish it wasn't in mine." He finished his water and set the glass in the sink when he felt her small hand resting on his arm.

He flinched. He couldn't help it, the way her touch stirred feelings in him that he had no right to feel. This time, she didn't step back. In fact, she slid her other arm around his waist, leaning against him as if she needed to comfort him.

"Annie, don't," he said. He wanted her to walk away—hell, to run away from him now.

"What's wrong? Please, Sean, tell me. I need you to come back to me, to be human again. Please." Her voice cracked. That moment when she fought to hold herself together always got to him.

He didn't even know how it happened. He was kissing her, his hands on her face, holding her to him, tasting her and all her sweetness, which he'd dreamed about having again for so long. He felt her hands on him, running over his waist and up his back as she stepped closer to him. He couldn't stop no matter how much he needed to. He was like a madman standing on the edge of a cliff, about to go over, and there wasn't a damn thing that was going to hold him back. He was free-falling right into Annie.

She was pulling at his jacket, and he pushed her hands away, grabbing the hem of her shirt and lifting it off. He reached around and unhooked her bra, kissing her as if she was his only source of air. He'd drown if he pulled away from her. He couldn't, he wouldn't. He was lost in her as if she was a drug. He undid her jeans, pushing them down with her underwear, and lifted her to the counter while she kicked off her pants. He didn't waste a moment as she undid the button on his jeans and wrapped her hand around him.

He held her hand as he kissed her again, deeper and then

down her neck as she tilted her head back, giving him all of her. She was on the edge as she guided him to her, and one thrust, one hard thrust, and he was inside her. Her arms linked around his neck, holding on to him as he pulled away and then slammed into her again.

"Sean, don't stop," she said.

He just held her there like that, feeling her all around him, her legs around his waist. God, he had waited so long for this, but he didn't want any of his damage to stain her—and it would if he kept going.

He rested his forehead to hers, pressed together, nose to nose. Her warm breath ghosted across his face as she ran her hand up the back of his neck, in his hair, and over his cheek and then pressed her lips again to his so softly, so sweetly. Sean knew without a doubt that he was a goner. There was no pulling away, no turning back, and he was damning her to hell with him.

CHAPTER 11

Annie swore she had died and gone to heaven—or close to it. She turned her head on the pillow, resting to face her husband, who was lying next to her in bed.

She closed her eyes, letting out a silent thank-you along with a sigh, so grateful that Sean was in bed with her again. When he lifted his arm up and rested his wrist against his forehead, it instantly had a knot tightening in her stomach. She could feel him distancing himself from her again.

"I know you're awake, Annie, and that sounded a lot like relief, but it shouldn't be," he said. "This was…"

She put her hand on his arm as she rolled to her side to face him fully, holding the covers up over her breasts. She was touching him, but the blankets were a barrier between them. She slid her hand over his chest, loving the feel of the soft hair that covered it. "Don't you dare say this was a mistake. It wasn't a mistake. I'm your wife. You say anything about not wanting me and I won't believe you. That was wonderful."

He lifted his arm away as he stared up at the ceiling and rolled until he was on top of her, taking her with him. The covers gone now, she could feel the desire between them.

"Hell, yes, I wanted you. Only a fool wouldn't want you. But whether I should want you is a completely different story. You're in me, but I've done and seen things I don't want touching you. It's too soon."

Annie wanted to push him to open up, but the wildness in his eyes was warning her not to. Maybe she'd pushed too far, and maybe he knew what she was thinking, as the next thing she knew, he was shaking his head.

"Don't," he said.

She spread her legs, sliding her heels up the back of his legs. The man wasn't immune to her; she could feel him fighting the pull. His arms were holding him above her, keeping his weight off her. He was so damn strong, but she was also prepared to pull out all the stops so he couldn't pull away. Using sex was something other women did, never Annie, but she was desperate, and she would. She ran her hands up his arms, loving the feel of the cut of his biceps, how he had the perfect shape. She appreciated the feel of his solidness as she traced a path up to his shoulders.

Sean shut his eyes for a second as he fought to gain control, but she was having none of that. She was done letting him pull away, so if she had to pull out every trick from her arsenal to seduce her husband, she was going to. Layer by layer, she was going to peel back all the scabs, scars, and hurt and find a way to connect with him again.

He wouldn't let her kiss him as he held himself up. Her legs, her feet slipped around his buttocks, holding herself there. Hell, no, she wasn't letting him pull away without a fight. After taking her hard and fast in the kitchen, he'd carried her upstairs, stripped out of his clothes, and taken her again. The last time had started out slow and tender but ended fast and hard. She was still a little sore, but she wasn't about to let that stop her.

"You don't want this, Annie," he said as he gave in a little and lowered onto one arm so he could press a kiss to her. His hand slipped back to unhook her legs from him.

"Yeah, I do. I've waited for this for so long, for you to come home, to come back to me. We had plans, Sean."

This time, he managed to unhook her leg, and he was suddenly off her, sitting on the side of the bed, about to get up, when she wrapped her arms around his neck to hold him there. Her breasts flattened to his back, and he groaned again.

"Don't fight it, Sean. Don't leave me here alone tonight. I want you back. I want my husband back."

He dropped his head into his hands. "Annie, I'm no good to you like this."

"Hey, I married you. Do you remember? For better or worse, and I'm sticking with you. Sean, I waited and left a great job, left everything to be here with you. I need you to fight for us."

He was still with her in bed, still sitting there even though she could feel how tightly he held himself, unable to relax, but he hadn't pushed her away. He was still there.

"If you only knew what I've done, you wouldn't be so quick to have me stay," he said. "You'd be horrified, and you'd hate me. I don't think I can bear how I know you'll look at me when you realize the man you married isn't who you thought he was."

This time, when Sean pulled away and got up, she let him go—because there was one thing Annie knew now that she hadn't this morning: Sean wasn't lost to her.

CHAPTER 12

The boat was shaking, bullets were flying, and there was screaming and shouting. Someone was in his face, yelling at him. He could hear an engine running. There was a hum. He remembered long dark hair. Then he was on him. There was clawing at his face, debris was flying, something hit him, but he didn't let go of the son of a bitch. He wasn't going to let go. He'd screwed up once; he'd be dammed if he let it happen again.

His hands were squeezing the windpipe, harder. He could feel the skin, the warmth of the body, the life he held in his hands and the ability he had to extinguish it.

"Sean..."

He heard it again. The voice was raspy as fingers clawed at his arm, but it barely registered. This guy was fighting back, but they always did. Then something hit his head, and he blinked, and he was cold, and his arms were bare. The room was dark, and the steel floor suddenly gave way to something soft beneath his knees. Where had his clothes gone, his uniform, the weight he always carried?

There was choking, hands slapping at his arms. He felt the sting of nails digging in, and in that moment he realized two things: He wasn't on a boat off the coast of Africa but on a bed, and this wasn't a man he was choking, it was a woman, and she was naked—and she looked so much like Annie.

He pulled his hands away as a tremble ripped through him, and he was shaking as she rolled off the bed and hit the floor, scrambling away from him. The light flicked on, and the bedroom was no longer in darkness as he stared at his bare hands. He could vaguely hear her crying and coughing in the distance, but she wasn't there. She'd left the room and run down the stairs.

What the hell had he just done? He was confused. He couldn't believe he'd hurt her. He'd been at war, at sea. It was just supposed to be a routine boarding, but everything had gone wrong, and it had been his fault.

He was naked as he sat on the edge of the bed. Then he heard her whimpering and crying, and she was talking to someone. "Annie," he said, starting out of the bedroom. The lights were on downstairs. He stopped and pulled on his jeans before starting down. She was in the living room with a blanket around her, still on the phone, staring up at him as he walked in. What gutted him was that the moment she saw him come down the stairs, there was fear in her eyes, terror, something he'd never, ever in a million years have expected to see. Her face was blotchy and red, her eyes swollen from crying, her nose running, and her neck red from where his hands had wrapped around her windpipe and squeezed.

"Oh, Annie, baby, you're hurt." He started toward her, but she instantly backed up.

"He's here now," she said. "No, he tried to choke me. I couldn't wake him…" She was yelling, her voice hoarse, and it sounded as if it hurt her to speak. She was crying and shaking.

"Annie, I'm so sorry! God, baby, let me see you. Let me help you. Are you hurt?" For a minute, he thought she was going to run. She was panicked, and she'd finally realized the danger he posed. Her hand was shaking as she handed him the phone, then pulled the blanket tighter around herself.

"Sean! Sean, this is Zac. What the hell happened?"

He could hear his friend calling out through the phone, but he couldn't find the words. He was mortified that he'd done something this heinous—to Annie! He loved her. What kind of monster hurt the one he loved?

"Zac." His voice sounded so odd. He choked on a sob. He ran his hand over his hair as he watched Annie, who was now standing across the room, tears running down her face, shaking, looking right and then left as if she needed to get out of there, away from him. He sucked in a breath to pull himself together.

"What the hell, Sean? I could barely make out what Annie was saying. She said you hurt her, you were choking her, tried to kill her."

"I—I..." He stopped. He couldn't get the words out. "I don't know what happened. I was dreaming. I think I was at sea. It was a boarding, a security check, and then bullets...and I don't know what happened."

"Diane and I are on our way," Zac said as Sean watched Annie run up the stairs to their bedroom and slam the door. He heard the lock click. It was worse than horrible that she felt she needed to lock him out, and what was worse was that the lock wouldn't keep him out if he really wanted in. Maybe she just needed that to feel safe. He'd give her that. He had to.

"Yeah, yeah, get over here. Please, help her. I should leave." He didn't know what to do.

"Is Annie going to be okay, or do I need to call the cops until we get there?" Zac had a way of talking to him that cut through all his self-loathing and hatred and everything that was closing in on him so that he couldn't breathe. "Yeah, of course she is. She's upstairs now. She's safe there, away from me. I'll stay down here."

"You do that. For your sake, Sean, she better be okay when we get there."

Sean stared at the disconnected phone in his hand and at the stairway, and it was then that it hit him: He didn't want this to be the end.

CHAPTER 13

Annie was huddled into a corner of the bedroom, staring at the chair she had fixed under the doorknob to keep the door closed. She needed it to stay there. She feared each second that passed that Sean might try to break through that door and finish her off.

Maybe she should have called the sheriff instead of Zac, but then, Diane was a cop. She'd send help, wouldn't she? Of course she would. She'd be okay. Everything was going to be okay. Maybe she was in shock over having the man she loved more than her next breath crouched over her, trying to strangle her, trying to kill her. Waking up unable to breath as his hands squeezed around her throat was something she could never have imagined. It was like a really bad dream that she couldn't wake herself up from. The bitch of it was that Sean had been warning her to stay away from him, but why? How could this have happened?

She heard a vehicle and then saw headlights as she raced to the window and looked out. A truck pulled up to the house, and its two doors opened and closed. They were here, Zac and Diane. She listened to the pounding on the front door. She heard the voices but couldn't make herself open the bedroom door. She was shaking, and her feet had suddenly become lead weights.

There were footsteps on the stairs. "Annie?" Someone was knocking on the door. "It's Zac. Open up."

She stumbled, shaking as she went to the door and pulled the chair out from under the knob. Unlocking the lock, she knew it wouldn't have kept Sean out if he wanted to get in. He could have broken through the door, and no matter how much she wanted to run, to live, she also knew that if he really wanted to, he could have killed her.

She was trembling when she saw Zac in his dark coat, taking in all of her. She must have been a sight, still holding that blanket around her. She'd never thought to put on clothes or her housecoat. Why hadn't she gotten dressed?

"Are you okay?" His hand was on her shoulder, and she was trembling and fighting tears she didn't know she had. She couldn't get a sound out as she choked back another sob. Her throat ached, her neck. It was so painful that it hurt to cry. Then his arms were around her, pulling her to him as he placed his hand on her head, just holding her. "Shh, it's okay. Can you tell me if you're hurt and what happened?"

He was walking her backwards toward the bed. Then she was sitting. "Let me take a look at you," he said. She was holding up the blanket, and he was looking at her neck, touching her.

"Is she okay?"

Annie heard Diane and looked up to see her in the doorway. Her short hair was a mess and sticking up everywhere. As she came closer, Annie was still shaking.

She tried to talk: "I..." she began, but it hurt.

"Don't talk. Just nod, okay?" Zac said, and Diane just watched her with sympathy and something else, something that let Annie know she was in charge.

"Is she okay?" she heard Sean say, and she couldn't help stiffening. He sounded so heartbroken, and she thought he was crying. It was that sound that nearly brought her to her knees.

"Sean, I'm okay," she said. Zac still had his hand on her throat, and Diane turned then as if to block Sean from coming closer. He was devastated. She could see it in his face. "Diane, it's okay," she said. Her voice was so rough, and it hurt to talk, but she needed to be able to reach Sean, to touch him.

He brushed Zac aside and was in front of her, holding her face between his hands, looking at her. "I'm so sorry, baby. I would never hurt you. You mean everything to me. Please believe that." He was so intense and upset and raw and real.

"I know you wouldn't." She clutched the blanket with one hand and touched his cheek, and he let her. He wasn't running or putting distance between them. He was here now, and he pulled her close and held her tight. She put her hand on his chest. "Sean, I can't breathe," she said. Her voice was raspy. He was warm.

"I'm so sorry," he said, and he pulled back.

She touched his chest, looking into his eyes and seeing his panic. "It's okay, Sean. I know you didn't want to hurt me. I know you wouldn't ever. It's okay. I'm okay. Look at me." She was the voice of reason. She had to be to reach him.

"Annie, I would feel better if Diane and I ran you to the hospital and got you checked out," Zac said.

She didn't want to go to the hospital, and she started to shake her head but winced. "No, I'll be okay. My robe." She swallowed, and it hurt. Sean pulled away and went into the bathroom to bring back her robe.

Zac and Diane were standing on either side of her, looking down at her, watching her, worrying about her. "You need to have a doctor look at you, Annie," Zac said. "You could have injuries to your trachea. You'll need x-rays. At best, there's swelling in your throat. Are you dizzy? Did you pass out?"

She was lightheaded, of course. "No, I didn't. It's okay, Zac. Sean…"

He glanced to Zac, who turned around as Sean helped Annie into her robe, belting it around her waist. "Annie, listen," he said. "Zac is right. You need to go to the hospital." He was touching her face, holding her again, and she shook her head, sliding her hands on his arms. Didn't he get it? She couldn't go to the hospital. There would be questions.

Even Diane got it. Annie could tell by her expression. "It's inevitable, Annie. Sean needs help," Diane said, not looking at Sean but at her.

Annie was shaking her head again. "Zac, Diane, no. This isn't the way."

"Annie, you're going to the hospital. End of story," Sean said. "I don't give a crap about me. It's you who's important."

"No, Sean," Zac said. He had reached out and was touching his shoulder, trying to get his attention. "Sean, listen to me. Annie is right. We go to the hospital, there's a police report. I know you don't care, but Annie does." Zac didn't take his eyes from her. He'd heard her, and she could tell with everything in her that he understood exactly what she was saying.

She nodded, and so did Zac.

"Diane, pack a bag for Annie," Zac said.

Sean squeezed his eyes shut, fighting tears. Then he nodded. "You go with Zac and Diane, Annie," he said. "Take her away from me."

"No, Diane will take Annie to our place," Zac said. "I'm staying with you."

Even though Annie didn't want to leave Sean, deep down inside, she knew that the help Sean needed was beyond her ability. She wasn't strong enough, because if she stayed, she also knew without a doubt that the next time she fell asleep, he would kill her.

CHAPTER 14

It should have been him out there with his wife, helping her into Zac's truck, but it wasn't, and he couldn't stand at the window, watching his wife drive away from him—even though that was what absolutely had to happen right now. He sat on the sofa, his face in his hands as he relived the horror in his wife's eyes. Annie, the woman he had promised to love and protect, now needed protection from him.

What was worse was that she was afraid of him. She feared for her life, and to see that fear in the face of someone he loved was worse than anything he could have ever imagined. For a long moment he sat there, waiting—for what, he didn't know. He was stuck in his head, reliving the feel of his hands around his beautiful Annie's throat as he squeezed the life out of her. The pain he was feeling was indescribable. He was terrified of who he'd become. It was the kind of pain that filled his heart, his soul, and the only way he believed he could ease it would be to grab a knife and pull the blade down his arm, slitting open his veins and allowing the blood to flow out of him. Only then would he find peace. For a moment, he considered how much better off Annie would be.

He heard the door close at the same time the vehicle

pulled away. His wife was gone now. He knew that, but it did little to relieve the giant hole that had been gouged into his heart. He knew, though, that Annie would be safer away from there.

Away from him.

He lifted his head, staring at Zac, who was watching him. Zac looked right and left before stepping down into the living room. He still had on his leather coat, his hands shoved into his pockets as he crossed over to the easy chair and sat across from Sean, still so close.

Zac didn't say anything for the longest time, just watching Sean and all his craziness. It was hard to sit under such scrutiny, to have his friend see the wickedness he'd hidden inside himself. It was something everyone had, a part everyone kept on a tight leash, hidden and under control. That was something he hadn't understood until now. But he'd lost control, and the beast he'd managed to keep locked away for so long was now loose. Zac could see it. Sean was embarrassed to be so vulnerable.

"You don't need to stay," he said. "You should go. Be with your wife, watch over mine."

Zac was already shaking his head. "Whatever you're thinking, get it out of your head. I'm not leaving. You think I don't understand where your head is, what you're thinking and planning?" Zac sounded really pissed as he leveled his hand at Sean. He didn't even try to hide how mad he was at him, furious, not about to pretend the deep end Sean had just gone over wasn't real.

"No, you think you're the first person to hit rock bottom?" he continued. "You think you're the only one to come back so fucked up that you hurt someone you love? But fuck, Sean, waking up and strangling your wife?" Zac was leaning forward, his arms resting over his knees. He rubbed his hands together. "Strangling Annie…fuck, Sean, you really took it to another level. Most guys just eat a bullet before it gets to that point." He leaned back, running his hand over his head as if he was trying to understand Sean.

Had Zac really just told him to kill himself?

"Give me the gun," Sean said. "I'll do it now."

"The hell with that. You think I'm going to waste my time cleaning up the mess of brains splattered everywhere? The bloodstains would never come out. Quite the pity party. What do you think that would do to Annie?" Zac was shaking his head. The fury he couldn't and wouldn't hide was directed at Sean like a laser. "You talk to your mom and dad yet?"

Where the hell had that come from?

"You call your parents," Zac said. "You talk to them. You've blown them off. I heard you on the phone when you called, leaving them a message that you and Annie weren't stopping in and were suddenly moving somewhere else. They had to be wondering what the fuck was up. Seriously? Come on, Sean. You think I didn't see the number of times your cell phone rang and you glanced at the number but didn't take the call? How many times did you let their calls go to voicemail? How many times have you deleted their messages?"

"What does it matter that I don't take their calls?" Sean said. "What am I going to say to them? Oh, yeah, the son who went off to join the army and thought he had everything figured out doesn't have it together, after all. There I was, thinking I would be the one kid who wouldn't ask my parents to foot the bill for a degree that would just add to the mountain of debt they already have from a brother who can't even keep his pants zipped and a sister who fucked off to LA and is doing God knows what, raking in the dough with all her government contracts. Did those two give a shit about our mom and dad as they took everything from them?"

Zac seemed so calm as he just listened to Sean rant. "What do your brother and sister have to do with your parents? So you want to play the martyr, is that what this is about? You chose the military. Whatever your reason, it doesn't matter. This isn't on them. This is on you, all of this."

Zac wasn't going to cut him any slack, because all of this came back to what he'd done. He hadn't been where he was supposed to be. He'd been out of position, and a team relied on all members being where they were supposed to be. It was haunting him, that one misstep where he'd gotten careless, choosing to open the door first instead of checking the stairwell. He'd known he was wrong the minute he did it, and now two men from his team were dead. Everyone knew he was to blame.

"They'll ask questions," he said. "Hell, Annie's been asking already, and she's the one person I can't hide from. But she can't know, and I can't lie to them. It's better if I don't call back."

Zac seemed to be considering something. "You have to tell Annie." When Sean went to add his *Hell, no*, Zac held up his hand. "Just listen to me. I'm not saying the details, because I know there's a lot of what happened that you can't talk about, but you need to tell her the gist of it. She'll understand."

Sean was shaking his head. There was no way in hell he was telling her, because Zac was wrong. Annie would hate him for the loss he'd caused, for sorrow of the women who were now widows. The thought of it brought him right back to where he'd been a moment before, how much easier it would be to just end it. He'd be gone and out of her life, unable to hurt her anymore, and she'd never have to know what he'd done. It seemed to be the best option, the best for Annie, because as bad as this was, having her hate him would be even worse. Right now, Annie was who he had to think of first.

"Killing yourself won't solve any of this, Sean," Zac said. "It's not an option. You think I wasn't there at one time with a gun to my head, looking to pull the trigger? I would have in that hospital. You have no idea how long I prayed to die during the months I was in that burn unit. I didn't think I would ever be able to get past what happened to my baby girl and to—" His voice caught. "But I did, and I'm now married to the best woman in the world, who loves me, and we're having a baby, a family. I got a second chance. You've got to want that for yourself."

Sean wanted to be happy for Zac, he really did, but right now he couldn't. "Zac, the difference between you and me is that you weren't responsible for Lizzy's death or for your baby's. That wasn't on you. You didn't screw up like I did, and you don't have blood on your hands like I do. You aren't the one so fucked up that you tried to kill the one person you love more than your next breath. I don't know how to explain what happened, how to make sense of all this. I would never hurt her. I was in my head, and I thought she was the enemy. I was squeezing the life out of the fucker who killed Lee and Hunter. I wanted to make it right, and I can't even imagine how I got upstairs, because I had left her in bed and gone downstairs. I must have fallen asleep. How the hell did I get upstairs? I've never sleepwalked in my life." Sean ran his hands through his hair, which was a mess. Nothing was helping him.

Zac was shaking his head. "I've heard a lot of things from guys who come back so messed up they're never right again. There was one guy I know who walked a mile in his underwear downtown, killed some guy he didn't even know. Woke up, had blood on his hands, didn't have a clue how he'd even got there. He was so freaked out over what he'd done. It's not an excuse. It's messed up when you don't know what you're doing."

"I'm fucked," Sean said. "I was always able to compartmentalize, to leave it where it needed to be left, to come home. Yes, there was always some adjustment, but Annie…" He couldn't finish. She had always been the breath of fresh air that grounded him. Her smile, her innocence, it helped. It always had, until now.

"Not this time," Zac added, watching him with such sympathy.

Sean just shook his head. "What the fuck am I going to do, Zac? She can't come back here. It's not safe here, not with me."

"Well, there's one thing, Sean. I'm not leaving you, not like this. You're going to get your head screwed back on. You're going to work through this. You did something, you screwed up, and you lost two men because you went right instead of left. You're not the first person in the military to do it, but you paid the price big time. You're done, finished. You need to move on, and you're not using it as an excuse. You need to look at yourself in the mirror, and you need to do right by Annie."

"How can I make this right when two good men are dead because of me? And now my wife...I almost killed her."

"Well, you'd better figure out a way to deal with it, because what happened to Annie tonight won't ever happen again," Zac said. "I guarantee you one thing: If there's a next time, it won't include you sitting here with me, trying to figure out your next move. You'll be staring at a set of steel bars for the rest of your life."

CHAPTER 15

Annie hadn't slept a wink. Being in another strange house, another strange room, she hadn't been able to settle. It was hard to relax in a place that wasn't hers. Of course there was also the fact that six hours earlier, she'd awoken unable to breathe with her husband on top of her, his hands wrapped around her neck, squeezing the life out of her. Now, as she relived it, she had to remind herself that the man on top of her, holding her down, hadn't been her husband.

Her hand went instantly to her throat, and it brought an ache as she remembered the fear of not being able to reach Sean. She swallowed past the lump, past the soreness that remained even though she'd taken the over-the-counter pain medication Diane had placed in her hand, swallowed with a glass of water after Diane had put her to bed. It had eased the painful throbbing to a mild ache, but it did little to touch the ache in her heart.

There was a tap on her open door. Annie winced as she turned her head.

"I guess that's my answer," Diane said as she lingered in the doorway, dressed, her hair damp. She was wearing a dark sweater and blue jeans and was holding a steaming mug. "I brought you some coffee."

Annie scooted up in bed, her nightshirt twisting around her waist, and plumped her pillow behind her. "Thank you." She reached for the mug, and it smelled heavenly.

"How did you sleep? Or, rather, did you sleep?"

Annie pulled her knees up and took a sip of the hot coffee. Diane sat at the foot of the bed. There was sympathy in her eyes as she looked at Annie.

"No, I tried but couldn't. Every time I shut my eyes and started to relax, I remembered, and…" She was afraid she'd fall asleep and not wake up this time. Even though that wasn't realistic, and Sean wasn't there, she couldn't shake the fact that every time she shut her eyes, she was afraid he would be. It wasn't a rational thought.

Maybe Diane knew, as she was shaking her head. "I can't believe I'm going to say this, because I don't believe in drugs, but I think maybe you need to take something to sleep. You have to rest. I'll talk to Zac. He can get you some sleeping pills." Diane was looking around the room at the soft peach walls. Annie loved the colors in Diane's house. Each room blended into the next. It was tasteful and easy on the eyes— comfortable colors that made a person want to just be in a room.

"What am I going to do, Diane?" She couldn't stay here forever. Zac needed to come home. Granted, it had only been one night, but she had a husband now who was over the edge. She had no job, and she was staying with a woman she barely knew.

"Nothing today. You're going to relax. You need to figure out what you want, what you need."

"And Sean?" she asked, because walking away from him wasn't something she knew she could do. She loved him, and she thought she'd reached him last night when he'd finally touched her, loved her. She had realized, though, in all her hours of tossing and turning, that all she'd done was reach a part of him he didn't want touched.

"Sean's okay. Talked to Zac a little bit ago. He's sleeping now. You do know Sean needs help, and it's the kind of help you can't give him."

Annie didn't say anything, because it hurt to think that she, his wife, couldn't help him through whatever this was, this haunting that had twisted him into the mess he was now.

"I get that you love him, that you think you can fix him, but you can't." Diane was very direct. "When Sean called Zac and then showed up here out of the blue, I didn't say anything to Zac because I trust him, but something was off. I saw it, and I know Zac saw it. I mean, he wouldn't leave me alone with Sean because he knew his friend was messed up. Before, we both thought it was just a matter of Sean getting through what he had to work through, and our biggest concern was that he might just leave."

"Diane, what happened to Sean? He won't tell me, but whatever happened, is that what messed him up?"

Diane was shaking her head. "Annie, I don't know what it is. Zac wouldn't tell me. I know they talked. It was pretty bad, but Zac told me to leave it alone. Whatever it was, I do know that for military reasons, Sean can't talk of it."

That was a fact Annie was clear on. It was a part of the military that she hated, the secrecy. But it was also a part she accepted. She couldn't help thinking of Zac, of what he'd been through. What it must have been like for him to get past his loss.

"Diane, Sean told me last night about what happened to Zac, to his baby, to…" *To the woman he felt betrayed him by putting herself in danger.*

"Zac doesn't talk about it," Diane said. "Yes, he told me because he wants kids so bad and he needed me to understand. I know it haunts him. It was a really big thing between us for a while. He'd asked me to marry him, but the baby, the whole baby thing almost ended it between us. I didn't want kids, not that I don't like them. It just wasn't on my list. But let me tell you, Zac wasn't going to back down. He's not a man that compromises—much," she added, and there was a hint of a smile.

"He sounds about as forthcoming as Sean."

Diane merely grunted.

"Diane, what am I going to do? What if Sean won't tell me what happened? I mean, he's pulling away, and I thought for a moment last night that I had cracked through that wall and finally reached him…and then this." She gestured to her throat as she felt herself tearing up. The last thing she needed to do was cry, which would make her already raw throat unbearable. So she breathed deep and then took another sip of coffee.

"He may never tell you, Annie. Don't expect him to open up, because first he has to find a way to deal with it himself."

"And what if he can't?"

"Then you need to be prepared to walk away."

That was the one thing she didn't want to hear. Maybe Diane knew, as she patted Annie's foot and then stood up and started out of the room.

"Diane," she called out. Diane stopped in the doorway, turning and resting her hand on the doorframe. Her diamond wedding band flashed on her finger. She didn't say anything as she waited for Annie. "If this was Zac and you were in my place, would you walk away?"

Diane just stared at her, then looked away for a minute before turning back. "But it's not Zac, and as difficult as he is, and God knows he has baggage that almost did come between us, Zac is not Sean. Right now, I'm thankful for that, because this is a choice I wouldn't want to make." She tapped the doorframe and appeared to be considering something, but instead of saying whatever it was she was thinking, she started to walk away. She then stopped as if she'd forgotten to tell Annie something. "I've got to go to work, so make yourself at home. Fridge is stocked with food. I'll be back at around six. If you need anything, I wrote my cell number on a notepad on the kitchen table. Call for any reason. Zac said he would stop in, too."

Annie didn't know how long she sat there in bed as she listened to the vehicle start and then pull away, followed by quiet. Instead of getting up, she rested her cup on the bedside table and then scooted down, pulling the covers up over her shoulders to try to get some sleep.

CHAPTER 16

"Wake up," Zac said.

Sean was sure he jumped as he blinked from Annie's bed, which he'd crawled into late last night. He would have rather slept on the sofa, because breathing in his wife's scent and knowing he was responsible for driving her away was agony. The sun was now streaming through the front window, and there was Zac, standing over him.

"You have to be at work, and so do I," Zac said. "You need to get your ass downstairs and help me find the coffee."

Sean's head ached, and as he sat up, he remembered clearly why Zac was there and Annie wasn't. "I don't know where Annie keeps it," he said. He stepped into his jeans and followed Zac down the stairs into the kitchen. Zac was looking a little rough. His shirt was untucked from his jeans, and he was barefoot as he rummaged through the cupboards.

"Annie looks after all that," Sean said. She actually looked after everything. He'd get up, and coffee was ready. She cooked, she cleaned, she looked after the home. He looked after her—or he had.

"Found it." Zac shook a yellow canister, popped the lid off, and slid the coffeemaker forward. The coffee filters were tucked behind it. Zac dumped the grounds in and poured the water, and Sean just stood back and watched.

"You talk to Diane this morning?" Sean asked as Zac dug out two mugs from the cupboard and set them on the counter, which was still stacked with unpacked dishes Annie had yet to put away.

"Yeah, I did. She put Annie to bed after giving her some pain medication. She was about to wake her. That's all I know. I'll stop in on my way to work and check on her."

"I'll go with you."

This time, Zac looked up, and it was easy to see he had a lot to say on the subject. Sean was wondering whether he would say no, and he wondered how far he could push. The fact was that it was killing him that Annie was over there and he was here and there was nothing he could do for her.

"I think that's a great idea," Zac said, the one thing he hadn't expected.

Maybe the surprise registered on his face. "Great. I thought you were going to tell me to stay away from her, that you'd keep me away. Not that I can blame you."

Zac didn't wait for the coffee to finish brewing. As soon as there was enough in the carafe, he filled the two mugs and handed one to Sean. "Unless you're asleep, I have no intention of keeping you from Annie. I just won't leave you alone with her right now. Not that I'm afraid you'll do something while you're awake, but I wouldn't want Annie to be afraid. You scared the hell out of her last night, and the only reason you're not sitting in jail right now is because she loves you and she called me first. You should know that my wife wanted to dispatch a unit to sit on you until we got here, but I convinced her not to."

What could he say to that, that he was grateful? He didn't know what he was, but there was something about the reality of daytime that cast a different light on things. Right now he wanted to swear it would never happen again, but he feared that was just talk, because there was little that had changed. He was barely holding himself together, and he didn't know if he could ever be the husband Annie wanted, the husband she needed.

"I'll get showered, and then I'd like to go over and see Annie," Sean said. He also needed to report to work, to a job he knew he could do well at, a job he was determined to do right.

"Yeah, just hold up, Sean." Zac took a swallow of coffee. "You need to find a therapist today, too."

"Oh," he said. He didn't know what he'd expected from Zac, but shipping him off to some shrink wasn't it.

"Whatever happened last night had you blacking out, Sean. Something triggered you." Zac gestured with his mug. "Obviously, you know it and I know it, and until you know what the problem is, what the trigger is, it's kind of hard to avoid it. Then what? You need to fix yourself, fix it. Would you just take a chance with Annie and hope it doesn't happen again?"

"Of course not. That would be crazy. I just want to make sure she's okay."

Zac took another swallow of his coffee but didn't say anything.

"Let me ask you this, Zac. With what happened with you, when you lost Lizzy and your baby, you were a mess. How did you pull it together?" Sean really did want to know, because he hadn't expected to find Zac married with a kid on the way, living in a small rural place in a nice house in the country, a house that screamed family and home. The only thing missing was a white picket fence.

Zac seemed to pull away for a minute and leaned back against the counter. "It never really goes away. You just learn to deal with it the best you can. Stick your crap here, deal with what you can, and the rest gets better. I went back to school, got a degree in forensics. I pushed through. But it never really goes away."

He really didn't know what to say to that. Maybe Zac understood a little.

"Until I met Diane, though, I didn't think it was possible for me to fall in love again—for me to hope." He put his mug in the sink. "Well, let's get going."

Whatever it was that lurked in the shadow of Zac's eyes had Sean wondering whether he was holding on to something more.

"Give me five to shower and dress," Sean said.

"Four minutes and I'll meet you outside."

That didn't leave Sean much time at all to get ready to see his wife. As he climbed into the shower, he realized this was the first time in the days since he'd arrived that he wasn't pushing Annie away. Maybe, just maybe, there was hope for him yet.

CHAPTER 17

Annie was reading the paper Diane had left when she heard a vehicle pull up. A car door shut, followed by the sound of another vehicle. She started to get up, glad she'd decided to climb out of bed and get dressed in a pair of sweatpants and a turtleneck when she hadn't been able to go back to sleep.

The front door opened. For a minute, she felt uneasy when Zac strode in.

"Hi, Zac. Thanks again for letting me—" She stopped when Sean walked in behind Zac. His eyes went right to her, and he stopped. His hesitation lasted just a fraction of a second. Then he stepped around Zac, toward her.

He didn't hesitate or try to avoid her, as he'd done every day and every moment since she'd arrived in Port Angeles. He was right in her space, looking at her with such remorse that she was sure her heart cracked open again. "Oh, Annie, I'm so sorry."

She was in his arms, leaning against him, the one place she'd wanted to be every day since he came back. She slid her hand up his chest, feeling him and his solidness, at the same time taking a look at him in his red jacket, dressed and ready to go to work. He'd even shaved.

He pulled the neckline of her sweater down and winced at the bruises she knew were vividly imprinted there. She'd seen it herself in the mirror, the black and purple that covered her neck. There wasn't a chance, for the next while at least, until the marks faded, that she could step out of this house without a scarf or turtleneck to hide the brutal assault.

"It's okay. It looks worse than it is. I'm okay." She touched his hand to reassure him and then noticed that Zac was behind the counter, not far from her, watching. It felt awkward. What could she say to the man she loved, who had, a few hours earlier, tried to kill her?

"So, Annie, I've talked to Sean about getting some counseling," Zac said. "I'm going to hook him up with a local doctor here who has been working with some other military guys."

"Oh?" She hadn't expected that. Sean was still in her space. He hadn't pushed her away. "Really, Sean? That's great. It is, right, Zac?" She was looking over to Zac, but Sean wouldn't take his eyes off her.

He was watching her so intensely, as if she were the only one in the room. "I would do anything for you, Annie, for you to be safe. You know that, right?"

"I know, Sean. I know you would never hurt me intentionally."

"It will never happen again, Annie. I promise you that."

How could he promise something like that? Even though she knew he truly believed what he was saying, she couldn't help the moment her hand slid up over her neck.

"How about breakfast?" Zac said. "Sean, Annie?" He was rummaging in the fridge. He'd pulled out eggs and then reached for a fry pan and put it on the stovetop.

"I can't," Sean said. "I have to go to work." He stepped

away from Annie, and the moment of just them in the room broke.

Zac reached for a banana from the fruit bowl on the counter and tossed it to Sean, who caught it one handed. "Eat something on the way, then. Call me when you're done," he said as Sean stepped so casually back to Annie before leaning down and kissing her as if this were just an ordinary day and he was kissing his wife goodbye. He pulled away and touched her face again. He could be so attentive at times. He could make her the center of his world.

"I love you" was all he said before he stepped back, waved to Zac, and left.

For a minute, she believed everything would okay as she looked over to the closed door and listened to his truck pull away.

"One night doesn't make him cured, Annie."

She hadn't even realized Zac was watching her as he cracked eggs in a bowl and then set it down, his hands resting on the counter as he gave her all his attention.

"I know that," she said. Of course she did, but something had happened between last night when Sean had taken her to bed and the terror of that morning. Whatever it was that had been holding her husband away from her had finally broken open. It may have unleashed all kinds of hell, but she believed in that moment, whether Zac did or not, that Sean was on his way back to her.

"Do you? Because all you saw was a man clawing his way back. He's desperate, he needs help, and making promises that it will never happen again is something Sean can't do. I really hope you do understand, because even though he may want to believe it won't happen again, the fact that it did happen and that Sean had no control over it should make it very clear to Sean and you that he has some serious work to do. Annie, he's only just started."

She wanted to argue with Zac. She knew her husband

better than him. She even started to say just that when Zac's cell phone started ringing.

"Zac here," he said. He was walking away, and she couldn't hear what he was saying as he left the room, leaving her alone with her thoughts.

"Annie," he said when he came back, "I've got to run. That's work calling." He was in the doorway and then gestured to the breakfast he'd started but had yet to finish.

"Go," she said. "It's fine. I'll clean up." She was having a hard time looking at him, because his scrutiny had a way of digging into places she didn't like others looking. It made her feel vulnerable, leaving her raw and exposed.

"Listen, about what I said…"

She didn't want to hear any more of the raw truth about her husband. "If you're about to tell me to stop hoping or that what I just saw with Sean now wasn't real, that my husband doesn't want me or love me or that he's a danger to me and himself, I don't want to hear it again." She looked away as he stepped closer.

"Annie, look at me." He was right in front of her—her husband's friend, Diane's husband, a man so together she wished he were Sean. She forced herself to look up and into the sympathy staring back at her. "I'm not saying any of that to you," Zac said. "Of course he loves you. This whole thing is tearing him apart. All of his erratic behavior is because of you, for you. Pushing you away, hurting you, as fucked up as it all is, Sean is just a man on the edge, fighting his way back. He really is at the point where it wouldn't take much to push him over. That's all I'm saying. Baby steps." He didn't linger then, stepping back. "I really have to go, but we'll talk more later."

Then he was gone, leaving her again to try to figure out where she and Sean would go from there.

CHAPTER 18

"Of course this isn't a mistake. Diane, I know what I'm doing," Annie said as she unlocked her front door and carried a paper bag of groceries into her house. She kicked off her sandals and stood for a moment in the front entryway, barefoot, taking in her home and everything that had changed. There was a beautiful hall table and a mirror now mounted on the wall, as well as a bench where she could store hats and gloves.

"Annie, listen to me. It's too soon. Stay with us for a while longer. You can't rush this sort of thing." Diane was behind her, but Annie was still blown away by the fact that her husband had set up her house, with new furniture in the dining room, and the kitchen had been unpacked and organized. She really was touched that he had gone to the trouble to turn this into a home for her.

"No, it's not too soon, Diane. It's been a week of staying in your guest room. Zac was here sleeping on the sofa for how many nights?" She put the grocery bag down on the cleared countertop, loving the feel of being back in her kitchen in her new house, a house she'd only lived in for three days. There was something about her own space, her place, that allowed her to be herself.

"Zac doesn't mind," Diane said. "It's fine, really."

This time, Annie looked over at Diane in her jean jacket and didn't miss the bulge where her sidearm was fastened to her belt. "The fact that you brought me home and felt the need to be armed is a little disturbing. For heaven's sake, Sean has bent over backwards for me. He's seeing that nice Doctor Banks. Did you know he's starting to tell me how he feels? But it's more than that. It's all those little things that I loved that he didn't do before. He's become so in tune to me. He's running the trails with me every morning, bringing me flowers, holding my hand when we walk, stopping to enjoy the little things like a small child playing in the playground or a puppy we see while walking. It's just that the old Sean was great, but I like my new Sean, who's showing me how much I mean to him."

Diane didn't seem to agree, as she crossed her arms, not looking away but showing Annie she could be just as stubborn. "For your information, I just got off work. I'm a cop. I wear my sidearm on the job. I didn't pack it because of Sean."

"Really?" Annie said. She knew that was a load of crap, considering that since Diane was pregnant, although newly, she was now on desk duty.

"Yes, it's kind of something I need to catch bad guys with."

Oh, that had Annie's attention. She still remembered the fight and standoff between Zac and Diane where he'd demanded she quit and she indicated that as soon as her boss found out, she'd be put at a desk. Maybe Zac had been right to worry that she wouldn't stay put.

"Diane, are you telling me you're still out in the field? You're not at a desk? I distinctly remember how upset Zac was when you said you wouldn't quit, and you assured him you wouldn't put your baby in jeopardy."

It was just a second, the flash of something in Diane's face that gave her away.

"You didn't tell your boss you're pregnant?" Annie said. She couldn't believe Diane of all people would pull something like that, especially after Zac's previous loss. It was something she knew, from Sean, still haunted him.

"I plan on it, okay?" Diane said. "It's just early. I'm not even six weeks. Anything could happen yet. I could miscarry, and if I've told my boss, I'll still be benched with no baby and no job. Once you're at a desk, it's damn near impossible to get back what you've earned—especially with all the doors I've had slammed in my face, having to fight to get respect, to earn my place in the good ol' boys club." She was shaking her head. She was stubborn—unreasonable, maybe.

"Diane, does Zac know?"

This time Diane's face flushed. She didn't need to say any more, and for a minute Annie wondered whether she was going to deny it or have some excuse. Then she shook her head.

"He's going to be mad."

Diane made a face that melted away all her attitude. She was just as vulnerable as all of them. "He's going to be more than mad. He'll think I betrayed him. He'll be hurt, and he'll start making demands."

"Well..." Annie wanted to say that Diane needed to talk to Zac, to make him understand, but how could she begin to reason with a man like Zac? He was much like Sean in so many ways.

"He has to trust me," Diane said. "I'm not Lizzy. I wouldn't put myself at risk, running into a war zone as pregnant as she was. That was thoughtless, stupid. It's not the same. We're not living in a war zone, where you're driving down the road and chances are really high that you could hit a landmine."

"Diane, I can only imagine how upset Zac will be, but you've got to know, losing his baby the way he did, he may not be able to take the chance. I like you, Diane, and I like Zac, and I think you're both great. The way you've stepped in to help me, to help Sean…you have no idea what your friendship means. I just don't want to see something like this come between you and Zac." For a moment, she considered shaking Diane to get her to see that she needed to bend a little for Zac on this.

Diane didn't say anything for a moment as she rested her hand on her gun. "I had to fight a lot of things to get where I am. I'm not ready to just pack it in. I need more time. I love what I do. I mean, why does a man get to keep doing what he's doing, but women have to give everything up? I don't know if I can do it." Seeing a vulnerable side of Diane wasn't what Annie had expected. She'd never seen this from Diane, not ever in the past week.

"You're human like all of us, Diane, but it's different, because you're not a stockbroker sitting behind some computer, working a nine to five job with the only danger being a paper-cut. You have a gun strapped to your side. Do you know what the statistics are of shootings and injuries in your line of work?" Annie knew. It was why policing and military were considered dangerous occupations. "I'm all for the right to equality, but if you continue with your job knowing the way Zac feels about it, you could be risking more, so ask yourself whether your job is more important than a life with Zac."

Maybe she wasn't being fair. Hell, Annie was still trying to have something normal and safe with her own husband—as if there was anything normal and safe with men like Zac and Sean.

"Sometimes it's not that simple, Annie."

"Diane, sometimes simple is what you have to make it be," Annie said. After all, wasn't that exactly what she was doing?

CHAPTER 19

Coming home to an empty house was not something Sean looked forward to doing. He loved his job with the coast guard in this part of the world. He liked the fact that he was working a job that would give him the sense of normalcy that he wanted, that he needed. It was a job that wouldn't take him away from Annie for weeks and months at a time.

The chance of coming across a threat had dropped, in all probability, by ninety percent. Okay, maybe eighty. Even though he was no longer patrolling seas filled with pirates and terrorists looking to blow them out of the water, unsavory criminals still used the water in the San Juan Islands to transport a number of illegal goods. More importantly, he was holding it together, not dreading each moment of every day, waiting for the other shoe to drop.

He set his keys on the entry table, sniffing the air, and could hear noise coming from the kitchen. "Zac, I didn't see your truck out front, but seriously, dude, you've got to pack it in with all this babysitting shit and go home and see your wife—" He stopped short when the prettiest sight in the world greeted him.

"Not Zac," Annie said. "Just your wife."

Two things in that moment left him speechless: Her smile and the way it lit up her face, and the fact that she was barefoot in the kitchen, wearing a simple sundress as she walked over to him to greet him. She rose up on her tiptoes and pressed a kiss to his lips.

"Hey, that's some greeting. What's this?" Not that he was complaining, but whatever she was cooking smelled fantastic. He sniffed the air in appreciation, and his hand went right to her hips, holding her there. It had been a long time since he'd been able to hold her like this.

"Dinner," she said. "I wanted to do something nice for you because I know you've being trying so hard, working so hard to make things right." She seemed so carefree and at ease. He had missed this so much from her. It was as if he'd been able to rewind the clock back to before his last tour, before things turned bad, before he screwed up. He didn't want to think about that, so he pushed it away.

"Do you have any idea what it means to me to come home and find you here? It's every man's dream to find his wife like this in the kitchen. I want you here in this house. This is your house. I picked it for you. It's my dream for us. You know, Annie, it feels like I hit pause, but I want to pick up where we left off, to start building our life together." He really did after hitting the bottom a week ago. He'd started seeing everything around him differently, even his family, the parents he'd pushed away—the two people who would be able to see how truly messed up he was.

She just smiled that amazing smile, lighting up her face again. It was the thing that had attracted him to her, and he swore it made her the most beautiful woman he'd ever seen, touched, had the pleasure of being with. "Dinner's almost ready," she said, and she went back to the cutting board, where she was slicing up vegetables for a salad. "So tell me, how was your day?" She looked up, and he could see the flash of worry. "Or am I not allowed to ask?"

"Of course you can ask." He leaned on the counter closer and watched her relax again as she went back to assembling a salad. "Interesting. One boat carrying three people collided with another boat carrying four. It was alcohol related. It never surprises me, the number of people who think it's okay to operate a boat intoxicated. Anyway, the one that hit capsized, dumping all three into the water. They're all lucky we got there in time. There were some serious injuries. They were all checked out at the hospital, and the operator of the boat was arrested."

Should he share with Annie the fact that the man had been three times over the legal limit and cared more about his boat than the two women he'd had on board, one of whom was reportedly his girlfriend? "Other than that, a quiet day," he said.

"Well, I have some news." The way she said it, he could see she was really happy about it.

"Yeah, what is it?"

"I got a job today," she said. "Well, part time, really, but it's a start. It's at that really nice resort close to the park, administrative assistant to the manager. The woman who has the current position is going on maternity leave…" Annie was still talking as she put the salad on the table, and Sean found himself in the fridge, pulling out a beer, taking off the cap, and taking a swallow. "Sean?" Annie came up beside him and touched his arm. He looked down at her and could see worry.

"That's about an hour's drive from here," he said.

"Well, more like forty-five minutes, but isn't it great? I mean, it's a start."

Didn't she get it? He didn't want her driving that long and that far. "I don't want you working. You don't need to get a job."

"Sean, I'm not—we're not…" She stopped. "I want this job. It's important to me. I've always worked."

How could he make her understand that he'd never liked her working when they lived on base in Florida? He had been away so much then that it wasn't fair for him to ask her to stay home, but things were different now. "Well, maybe you shouldn't be working anymore. Do you remember, before I left, we were talking about starting a family? You were ready, and maybe I'm not too keen on you starting some career here and then our family comes second."

"Oh, no, you just hang on a second, Sean. We have a lot of steps to work through, the two of us, before family comes in. One is the fact that I just got home. We're taking baby steps. We're at A, and you're fast tracking us all the way to Z."

Had she really said she had just gotten home?

"Yeah, I'm home," she added with a teasing smile.

"You've moved back in? No more staying at Diane and Zac's?" Could this really be true? He finally had his wife back?

She smiled again, slipping her arms around his waist, resting her chin on his chest, gazing up at him. "See? We're at the first step. I'm home."

"Oh, thank God." He squeezed her to him, kissing her again. "Oh, baby, you have no idea how much I missed you. Everything is going to be okay now, I promise," he said again as she sighed softly in his arms. As he said it, he needed to believe he could do this and everything would be okay—because what he feared more than anything was screwing up again. This time, if he did, he might never get Annie back.

CHAPTER 20

Dinner had been spectacular. Although the food had tasted great, it was even better to be sitting with her husband at the table, sharing a meal and talking. Everything felt almost normal. Sean had even helped her clean up, wash the dishes, and put the leftovers away. Not that he hadn't before, but he was more attentive to her needs now, to everything about her.

Annie was sitting on the bed after soaking in the tub, rubbing lotion on her legs.

"I'm going to grab a shower before bed," Sean said as he walked into the bedroom, pulling off his shirt and dumping it in the clothes hamper.

"Did I hear the phone?" Annie said. She thought she had when she'd been in the bath, and she had just assumed it was Zac or Diane checking up on them.

Sean stopped in the doorway of the en suite and flicked on the lights. "Yeah, it was Mom phoning."

She hadn't expected that. Sean hadn't spoken to his parents in…she didn't know how long. "I didn't know you were talking to your parents again," she said. They had to be wondering what was up with him since the move.

"Everything's fine, Annie. I've talked to them a few times this week. They want to come out and see us. Dad's hired help and is working fewer hours at the firm. They're talking about buying an RV and doing some traveling, seeing their kids."

Well, this seemed really normal. This was great, the fact that he'd reached out to his parents. Maybe Zac had been wrong, because Sean was really pulling it together. "That sounds nice," she said. "I'd love to see your parents." She heard the water turn on in the shower and watched as her husband stripped out of the rest of his clothes and dumped them into the laundry hamper.

"They're going to head up and see Tom again, too. His wife is due in a few months, and they've been picking up my niece and nephew and taking them up to see him in Manhattan every weekend. Mom's tired." Sean was shaking his head.

Annie knew it bothered Sean how insensitive his brother had been, taking a new job in a Manhattan hospital and walking out on his wife, who was pregnant with their third. Tom had shocked the hell out of the entire family by hooking up with an ER nurse he worked with. From the sidelines, Annie had seen how the family had taken sides.

"You talked to your brother?" she called out as Sean climbed into the shower. She got up and walked into the bathroom to put the lotion back in the cupboard. She could see her husband through the glass door, washing himself.

"No, nothing to say. Do you really think I want to listen to his excuses, how he suddenly met the love of his life, his soul mate, and the past ten years with Doreen meant nothing? That he could just walk out like that and not look back..." Sean turned off the shower and opened the door, and Annie handed him a dry towel. "Thanks, babe."

This was so normal, talking here in the bathroom about family as Sean dried off. She had missed this, missed him.

"Well, he's still your brother." She wanted to point out that Sean and Tom had been so close at one time, talking every Sunday when Sean was home.

"No, not interested in talking with that dumbass until he faces up to his responsibilities and goes home to his wife. I'm with Susan on this."

Sean's sister was as stubborn as Sean, except she'd been a lot more verbal with what she thought of Tom walking out. She had, in fact, been Doreen's biggest supporter.

"It must be hard on your mom and dad. It sounds like they're stuck in the middle."

Sean tossed the damp towel in the laundry. "Their choice in the matter. They shouldn't be playing referee between Tom and Doreen. Tom walked out on his family, his kids. Tom should be the one going to see them, not having Mom and Dad bring them to New York every weekend to make it easier for him. It's just not right, Annie."

Then her husband, her very naked husband, walked toward her and pulled at the towel she had wrapped around her. "How about less talk about my family and more about just us." He pulled the towel from her and tossed it to the floor, then scooped her up in his arms. She squealed as he tossed her a bit. "Or less talking, period," he added as he laid her on the bed and covered her with his body.

His breath was warm as he kissed her, taking his time to do it right. If there was one thing she loved about Sean, it was that he knew how to kiss. Not many men could brag about something like that. It was one of many qualities about Sean that she loved—and she loved kissing him, touching him, being under him when he made love to her. With Sean, it could be fast and hurried or slow and gentle, but she was always left feeling as if she'd been well loved. There were times where he took his time to explore her body, to taste it, touch it, tease it, but not tonight. He had a need that seemed urgent as his hands traced her hips and legs and then spread her wide. Then he was inside her, running his hand over her rounded cheeks, holding her. "I've waited so long to feel you again, baby, to be inside you," he whispered before kissing her again.

He was tasting her, touching her. She wanted it to last as he filled her over and over. It was wonderful and beautiful, and she felt closer to her husband than she had been in a long time. It was frantic and wild, and she cried out as she felt him fill her with his warmth, with part of him. Then he collapsed with all his weight on top of her. She ran her hands down his back, feeling him still inside her, and then he stirred, groaning with pleasure as he kissed her neck and her ear.

"I missed you, Annie," he said when he rolled off of her, his arm around her, pulling her with him until she was lying on top of him as if he was her bed, a very hard bed that she could easily and comfortably sleep on.

He ran his hand over her bottom, touching every part of her. She listened to his heartbeat slow until it matched the beat of hers. It was a rhythm she loved, the rise and fall of his chest, the sound of his breath in and out. "And maybe, if we're lucky, we can start our family now, too," he said.

If any words could rip away the haze of fantasy, it was those ones. As far as he'd come and as good as things seemed right now, bringing a baby into this was exactly what shouldn't happen. As she shut her eyes, she also knew that it was also a very real possibility. She listened, thinking a little too much as his breathing evened out and he relaxed beneath her. She knew she'd made a very big mistake. It was the panic that hit first.

"I'm so sorry," she cried out as she pushed away from Sean. She was standing beside the bed, and he was now sitting up, reaching for her. Of course he was confused. Hell, she was freaking out, and for a minute she couldn't breathe. "I can't do this. I'm scared to go to sleep. I'm so sorry. I'm not strong enough. I thought I could do this, but I'm scared."

"Baby, please, no. I won't…it won't happen again."

She wondered, as she stared at the panic in his eyes, whether he truly believed that or he was saying it because he wanted to believe it. Then he was reaching for her as if that would make everything okay.

"Please come back to bed," he said. "Just let me hold you."

But she couldn't. She shook her head, stepping away. "No, Sean, please, no!" She grabbed her robe and held it up in front of her. "I thought I was ready, but lying there on top of you, I want it so bad to be just you and me. Then you start talking about a baby and bringing one into the world, and I can't do that, Sean. I can't take a chance of waking up to find you on top of me again, trying to kill me. I can't do it."

It killed her to see everything they'd just accomplished disappear. What was worse was that the hope in his eyes, which had been there from the moment he'd stepped into that kitchen and seen her, had disappeared. She felt horrible because she was responsible, as if she'd just blown out a candle, but the fact was that she was terrified, and she remembered what Zac had said, reminding her that Sean wasn't ready. She heard him in her head again, and that had her pulling on her clothes and reaching for the bag she'd just unpacked earlier that. She knew she had to leave.

CHAPTER 21

She had survived five days post Sean, and now she was moving into a small apartment closer to her work in neighboring Sequim. Of course Diane and Zac had protested, but she'd plastered on a smile, curving her lip and saying in a matter-of-fact way that no, she was done. She was moving out and on with her life. She had to, after that heart-wrenching night when she'd left Sean even after he'd pleaded for her to stay. She'd packed a bag, unable to stop the tears.

Maybe Sean had understood that no amount of pleading or begging was going to get through to her. The fact was that she loved him so deeply, and she knew he knew it, but her fear of him had finally gotten through.

He had slipped out of the bedroom, gone downstairs, and picked up the phone. He'd become calm, a voice of reason against her hysteria. She hadn't expected that or for him to call Zac and ask him to come and pick her up. She had stood there in shock, listening as her husband, the man she loved, helped her pack to leave him. Then he'd reached out for her with tears in his eyes when they heard Zac pull in. She, of course, had gone into Sean's arms, and he'd just held her for a minute before walking her out the door.

He'd kissed her goodbye five days ago after lifting her suitcase into Zac's pickup, kissed her again when she was in the truck, and said the one thing that had her doubting everything: "You go. Be safe."

And she had.

She had left Sean.

"You're sure about this?" Diane asked as she wandered through the furnished one-bedroom apartment Annie had rented.

"If I said yes, it wouldn't be honest, now, would it?" Annie put down her purse on the small dinette table, taking in the dismal place and wishing it could be any other way.

"You talked to Sean?" Diane started into the galley-style kitchen and opened cupboards filled with four of everything: mugs, glasses, plates, bowls.

What could she say to Diane, that she had called every day wanting to talk to him, to see how he was? She'd left more than a dozen messages and he hadn't called her back once. What had she done? Maybe he hated her now.

"He won't take my calls. If it weren't for Zac telling me he's seen him and talked to him and knows he's doing okay, I'd be thinking the worst and worrying all the time, more so than I am now."

"Where do you want this, Annie?" Zac came in carrying two of her suitcases.

"Just in the bedroom, Zac. Thank you." She gestured to the small bedroom, which had a reasonably comfortable double bed and a plain brown dresser.

"Thank you again, Diane. I didn't expect this from you and Zac. I mean, you've gone above and beyond." She treasured these friends of Sean's.

"Of course, but I wish you would reconsider. You really can stay with us a while. This seems a little rushed, Annie."

Diane had said very little to Annie after that first night she'd arrived back with Zac. Maybe she'd understood, or maybe she'd expected Annie to come back as she had. It had been hard, and she'd given Annie the space she needed.

"It's time," Annie said.

"What's time?" Zac said as he appeared behind Diane, running his hand over the flat of her stomach, which had a slight bulge. The man was certainly possessive, and as Diane leaned back against her husband, responding to him, Annie realized she loved every moment of his possessiveness even though she would deny it. She realized that people got it wrong. Men like Zac needed complexity in a companion, and it took a strong woman to be with a man like Zac.

"Time I stop using you two as a crutch and learn to stand on my own two feet," she said, watching as Zac held Diane to him with both hands as if he had no intention of letting her go. "Besides, you two need space."

"Annie, I told you you don't need to go, right?" He was resting his chin on the top of Diane's head, glancing down at her.

"Annie needs some space of her own, Zac. She's knows she's welcome to stay." Diane patted his hand. "Why don't you go grab the rest of the boxes and bring them up?"

Zac kissed Diane on the cheek. "There's only one more." He moved away but linked his fingers with Diane's as if touching her was something he needed to do. "You know Sean offered for you to take the house. He wants you to have it."

Zac had mentioned it a few times to her, and she really loved that Sean would leave for her, but she couldn't do that. "Sometimes a fresh start is important and new surroundings are needed," she said.

Maybe Zac didn't agree with her, but he didn't argue, either, as he left the apartment. Diane glanced over her shoulder as he went out.

"A place where the memories aren't going to drown you," Diane said. Boy, the woman really did understand.

"Yeah," Annie choked out, refusing to cry in front of anyone anymore. "Okay, stop talking about Sean and me and this move. I need to think about something else. Let's talk about you." She watched the surprise on Diane's face.

"Nothing to say, really." The woman could clam up tighter than anyone Annie had ever met. Not the typical woman, that was for sure.

"You forget I've been sharing a house with you and Zac for almost a week, and I know you haven't told your husband you're still not working a desk."

A clatter behind them made Annie jump, and Diane shut her eyes and sighed. Annie couldn't believe she'd just outed Diane. She wasn't one of those loose-lipped women, and she would do anything right now to pull those words back into her mouth and shut it.

"Zac, I..." she said. What the hell was she going to say as she stared at Diane, who had every right to be furious with her?

"You're not at a desk? Are you still going out in the field every day?" Zac's voice had become so low that it was almost deceptive. Annie found herself stepping in front of Diane, maybe in a foolish attempt to take some of the heat from her.

"Zac, calm down," Annie said.

"Annie, move out of the way. You think I'm going to hurt my wife?" Zac was almost shouting at her.

"No, I'm thinking you may have misheard what I was saying. Before you jump to conclusions—"

Diane put her hands on Annie's shoulders and moved her to the side. "I appreciate the sentiment, Annie, really, but don't go digging another hole because I screwed up." She looked over to Zac then. "I'm sorry. I kept meaning to say something, but I also know it's too early, Zac. Anything could happen to the baby yet. I'm still in the first trimester. I'm not even showing."

Zac leaned in so close to Diane that for a minute, Annie

thought she'd step back. To her credit, she didn't. "I told you to quit. You know how important this is to me, Diane. You're a cop who chases down bad guys and thugs who carry guns, and some of them want to hurt you or kill you for kicks or just to get away from you. They're all desperate."

Had Diane really just rolled her eyes? Annie had stepped away, watching Diane with her overbearing, very alpha husband, who still had some very serious issues about his pregnant wife. "I know that, but I'm careful. As soon as I'm showing, I will be at a desk."

"You'll be at a desk now, because I'm going to pick up the phone and call Green and let him know you're pregnant, and you're now benched or I'll rain holy hell down on that department."

"Zac, do you know how long it took me to get respect, for them not to see me as weak? I had to claw my way through the old boys club to get where I am." Diane wasn't going to back down.

"I know everything you've had to claw your way through, Diane. I know what you've had to overcome and what makes you who you are. You're not weak, you're strong, the strongest woman I know. It doesn't matter what those assholes think or believe."

Annie couldn't believe the tenderness coming from Zac now. She had half expected him to demand and then stomp around yelling if he didn't get his way, but instead he was using logic and reason and love. Her heart did a flip. Maybe Diane hadn't expected that, either, as she shut her eyes for a second as if she needed to digest what he'd said. When she opened her eyes, she looked at him like a woman in love.

"Nothing's going to happen to the baby," Zac said. "This baby is going to be loved." His face was so close to Diane's that they were almost touching, his hands around her waist, holding her.

Diane grabbed his jacket with both hands and walked into his arms. "Okay."

Annie wasn't sure she'd heard Diane right, but Zac was, as a smile touched his lips. It was so faint, but she realized the smug bastard already knew. As Annie leaned back against the wall, watching, she also realized Zac knew exactly what to say to his tough-as-nails wife to get her to concede.

CHAPTER 22

"Have you called Annie?"

Sean was in his backyard, grilling steaks on the barbecue, enjoying some time with Zac, who was leaning against the rail of the deck. "No. You want sauce on your steak?" he asked as he poured barbecue sauce on his and then sprinkled it generously with garlic salt.

"No, don't ruin those New York cuts. Those set me back forty buck. Maybe I should take over," Zac said, and Sean wanted to smile, because Zac was one of the cooks who tended to come in and take over completely. This time, he'd conceded and let Sean man the grill.

"How is she?" he asked even though it was killing him to have to ask his friend how his wife was doing.

"She's good. You should call her," Zac said again.

The problem was that the more time went past, the easier it was not to call. It didn't hurt any less that his wife had chosen to leave and never look back, though. Yes, she'd called every day for him the first week, and he'd sent every one of those calls to voicemail.

He shook his head again, taking another swallow of beer. "No, that ship has sailed. Saw a lawyer today."

A divorce lawyer was something he'd never pictured for him and Annie, but even though it killed him, walking in there to the lawyer and starting the process to end his marriage to the only woman he'd ever loved, he knew he was doing the right thing. It was right for her. It was better for her to set her free.

Zac cursed behind him. "Seriously, Sean, come on. What are you doing?"

"She take that money I gave you?" Sean asked again. Every week, he made sure Zac left with a check for Annie. He'd give her everything he owned, everything he had just so she'd be okay.

Zac nodded. "Took some convincing, like it does every time. She doesn't want to take your money, Sean. She's working full time now at that hotel. She seems to like it. You should call her, talk to her."

This time, Sean turned around, holding the tongs. This was the third time Zac had told him to call Annie in the space of five minutes, and it wasn't lost on him that something was up. "Look, if you have something to say, spit it out. Otherwise, drop it. Annie's better off without me."

"Is she? You sure about that?" Zac was really pushing it.

The fact was that he'd kill to see Annie, and he'd lost count of the number of times he'd made himself turn around when he found himself driving to Sequim, to the small apartment Annie was renting. "Is there something up that you keep pushing this? I'd really like to know, because if there isn't and you're just trying to torture me, well, stop it. You think I wouldn't cut off my right arm to have her back here? I would, but I can't, because the last time she was here and I was holding her and loving her, she freaked out. That panic and fear on her face is something I never want to see again, all because she was so scared to go to sleep with me. I'm the one man who's supposed to protect her from everything, everyone, and she's terrified of me. Do you have any idea what that did to me? It wasn't something she was just going to get over. She's truly frightened of me."

Zac looked away as if he was trying to find some words of wisdom to share with Sean. Sean really wished he would. "You still seeing the good ol' doc?" Zac asked him.

Dr. Banks was who he'd called the night Annie left. The man had driven in and met Sean at his office. He'd never shared that with Zac, but even the doctor, as of late, had been encouraging Sean to reach out to Annie.

"My wife is lost to me, but at least I'm getting my head screwed on straight. Talked to Mom and Dad, too. Tom and Doreen had another girl. They're working things out. Apparently he's left Manhattan General, gone back home to try to fix things with Doreen." He still wondered what it was that had made his brother walk away from his family the way he did. Maybe it was time he picked up the phone and called his brother, talked to him again.

"Good for Tom," Zac said.

There was something about Zac, the way he seemed to be holding on to something, that bothered Sean. "Are Diane and the baby okay?" he asked. He hoped so, considering this baby meant everything to Zac, as did Diane.

"Diane went on maternity leave today. It was her last day. Should have seen her. She's so beautiful, especially now she can't seem to tie her shoes anymore. Even Green, who she's butted heads with for years, was surprisingly nice to her, helping her up from her chair. He even threw together a little party in the squad room. It was nice."

"Didn't you tell me you were getting her to quit? I could have sworn your exact words were 'As soon as you have my baby, you're at home. You aren't playing cop anymore.' Weren't those your exact words?" He knew he was teasing Zac, especially since the topic of Diane going back to work after the baby had set Zac in a tailspin the likes of which Sean had never seen.

"We're compromising right now. She's taking a year off after the baby to stay home and be there. She's doing this for me even though I know she's absolutely terrified of being a mother, even though she won't admit it." Zac gestured with his beer to not ask. "We all have stuff we hold on to, Sean. Diane just hasn't shaken all hers off yet, but she's working on it."

Sean wanted to ask because he knew there was something in Diane's past that even Zac wouldn't talk about. Bad family or something. "Hope you're right. She's a good woman. So how did she get you to compromise? Since when do you compromise on anything, Zac?" He turned back to the barbecue and flipped the steaks one last time.

"Let's just say I know Diane, and after she's been home with our baby for a year, there's not a chance in hell she'll go back to work as a cop."

Sean realized Zac was serious. "So what happens if you're wrong and she does decide she doesn't want to quit being a cop?"

Zac gestured to the grill with his chin. "Won't get there, I told you, but if it does, I'll think of something else. Those steaks are done. Get them off the grill and plated before you burn the crap out of them."

Sean realized that Zac wasn't beyond pulling out all the stops to protect his family. As he turned off the grill and plated the steaks, he found himself yearning for what Zac had: a wife with a baby on the way, a family of his own.

CHAPTER 23

"Can you believe Green arranged this? I mean, who would have thought he'd have any idea what a onesie is?" Diane was holding a cute cotton undershirt, a sleeper, and diapers, rummaging through all the baby gifts she'd been given. From the stacks on the sofa and table, it looked like she wouldn't have to do laundry for weeks.

"I can't believe you got everything you need for the baby from one shower. Impressive," Annie said as she thumbed a very pretty little pink dress. "You're having a girl?" She hadn't heard Diane or Zac mention that they knew the sex of the baby.

Diane rolled her eyes. "Jeanette down at the station has six boys but always wanted a girl. She said she's convinced I'm having one because of how high I'm carrying. I think she honestly believes that by giving me a dress, she's going to make it happen."

Annie took in the size of Diane's pregnant belly, which was so large she looked as if she was ready to give birth. In fact, Diane was finding it more and more difficult to get up from the sofa or easy chair. Zac had been extremely attentive to Diane's needs. Annie envied her.

"So what are you going to do if it's a boy?" she asked. It was a cute dress, but kind of a waste if so.

"There are so many baby clothes here. It'll just be one more thing in the closet the baby will probably never wear. I mean, look at all these outfits! Completely impractical, too." Diane let out a sigh as she finished folding the baby's things into two piles, placing one on the coffee table before walking over to the easy chair and lowering herself into it. Diane did not wear dresses, but today she was wearing a cotton maternity skirt that draped past her knees, pale green with a matching shirt. It made her look amazing. It could have been the cut, as it had a slimming effect, and the color really brought out her eyes.

"You're pretty quiet over there. Is everything okay?" Diane asked her. "You know Zac and I have been kind of worried about you."

"I'm fine. Just in my head, is all. Sean is divorcing me."

There, she'd said it. It was the one thing she'd never expected to happen, even though it was the logical step. It had been months since she'd left. She'd cried every night, moving through stages of sorrow and sadness about a life without Sean, and now it was a reality she had to face.

"Oh, Annie, I'm so sorry. Have you talked to Sean? I can't believe he would divorce you, especially now." Diane was frowning and started to scoot forward in her chair.

"Where are you going?"

"I'm going to call Zac. He's over at Sean's now. Picked up some steaks and he's having dinner there."

"Well, why aren't you with him? I'm keeping you here. You should go," Annie said, because she was really feeling like the odd man out. She was alone, and she didn't really know much of what had been happening with Sean.

Diane gave up trying to get up and gestured with her hand to the phone on the table by the door. "Grab the phone and bring it here. And no, I'm not supposed to be there. This is kind of Zac and Sean's night, boys' night. They hang out for a few hours—more so Zac can make sure he's okay, I think. It's easier for Sean if I'm not there. He can talk with Zac about things he could never talk about otherwise. Besides, Zac has been hovering a lot. I really do need some time without him."

Annie reached for the phone, feeling awkward. "Diane, I know I told you I didn't want to know, but how is Sean doing?"

"Do you really want to know?" Diane asked. She could be so intense sometimes, the way she watched people. Annie was positive the woman was so perceptive that she could peel back the layers that hid all her vulnerabilities and secrets.

"No. I know I've never asked. He crosses my thoughts so often in a day that it was hard to function, but I've pushed through it so I can get up in the morning, go to work, and get through the day without that gigantic ache pressing down on me so much it hurts to breathe. Having you tell me about him would bring him back into my head more than he already is. I know I'd do something foolish and end up back in front of his house, knocking on the door, when we all know I can't be there, so why torture myself?"

She waited for Diane to say something, but all Diane did was fold her hands over the baby she carried. "Annie, you know I want you to be safe. I want you happy. If you want to know about Sean, ask me. If you don't, that's fine, too. Have you thought about calling him, talking to him?"

"And saying what, Diane?" She didn't hand the phone to Diane as she walked to the window and caught the flash of daytime running lights, then Zac's truck pulling in. She turned from the window as she listened to the door of his truck close. "Your husband's home," she said. She walked over and set the phone back in its cradle before reaching down for her purse, which she'd tucked on the floor beside the sofa. "I should go."

The front door opened, and she didn't miss the look of

surprise on Zac's face. "Annie, I didn't know you would be here. How are you feeling?"

She shrugged as he walked to her and squeezed her shoulders before setting eyes on his wife. Lord, the man was absolutely territorial over Diane right now. He stalked toward her, rested his hands on her chair arms, and kissed her long and deep. "Did you eat?" he said.

Annie wanted to sneak out and wondered if they would notice. At times, as of late, it was hard being around the two of them, considering how attentive Zac was to Diane's needs, whether she wanted him to be or not.

"Was thinking of ordering a pizza for me and Annie. Annie?" Diane called out as Zac stood and moved to the side. The expression on his face was pure disapproval.

"No, I should go," she said, even though she had nothing and no one to go home to.

"Don't be silly," Zac said, "and forget the pizza, Diane. Both of you should be eating far better than that. I'll put something together." Zac pulled off his leather coat and carried it to the hall closet, standing close to Annie. "Come on, Annie, stay. Besides, I wanted to talk to you about a few things."

Now what could be on Zac's mind that he wanted her to stay and talk about? Probably nothing that Annie wanted to hear. She found herself looking to Diane, who had been in her corner from the moment she left Sean. This time, the expression on her face as she connected with Zac made Annie feel as if something had been discussed between them.

"Zac, I really appreciate all you've done for me…"

"Annie, stop it. Look at you." He was shaking his head, touching her shoulder again. "It's time you talked to Sean. You can't wait anymore, Annie. Things have changed. It's time, Annie, and he's not the same. He's worked so hard these past few months to pull himself together. And that baby you're carrying…" Zac gestured to her expanding waistline and the baby she could no longer hide. "He needs to know. He has a right to know because things have changed—for him and for you."

"Zac, you promised you wouldn't tell. You know he's not ready."

Zac was now shaking his head, his lips firmed to a fine lie. "I know what I said, Annie, but as with everything in life, things change. If you don't tell him, I will, because your reasons for keeping Sean in the dark—well, they no longer apply."

Annie was now looking between Diane and Zac.

"Zac's right, Annie," Diane said. "I think you need to hear him out."

Annie hesitated for a minute, glancing at the door. She could walk out and not look back. Then she looked over to the sofa, where she could sit down and listen to what Zac had to say. She realized as she thought about the man she loved, the father of her child, that whatever Zac needed to say, it was time she listened.

CHAPTER 24

The front door bell was ringing again. "I'm coming," Sean shouted as he wrapped a towel around his waist after climbing out of the shower. The doorbell rang insistently a third time. "Geez, can't a man even enjoy a shower?" Sean muttered as he hurried down the stairs with the towel hanging low on his hips, running another over his dripping hair. When he pulled open the door, he saw her.

Her back was to him. She'd cut her hair, all those long waves gone, and then she turned around. She was even more beautiful than he remembered, standing there in her black fall coat, and he had to fight the urge to touch her.

"Annie." His throat jammed as he stared into the blueness of her eyes. Then he noticed the tiny faint lines around her eyes and mouth that hadn't been there before.

"Sean, can I come in?" She sounded hesitant, unsure. Just watching her brought a flood of memories of their months apart, the fear in her eyes, and the reason she'd left.

"I don't know if that's a good idea," he said, but he stepped back, opening the door wide.

She had her hands in her pockets and her purse over her shoulders as she stepped inside, and he shut the door behind her. "I got you out of the shower," she said. Her gaze lingered on his towel, and he sensed her awkwardness.

"Listen, why don't you make yourself comfortable, and I'll go put some clothes on?" he said. He watched as she went down into the living room and noticed her surprise at the changes he'd made.

"What happened to all the furniture?"

What could he say to her? He'd sold everything but the sofa. He'd have sold that, too, except it was the only thing he could sleep on at night since being unable to climb back in the bed where Annie had last been. He was done torturing himself. "Sold it. I'll be right back."

Sean hurried up the stairs and into the bedroom, reaching for his jeans and T-shirt and pulling them on. Then, because he needed another minute, he took a pair of socks from the drawer and sat on the made bed. He needed more time before he could pull it together to walk back down the stairs and see Annie. What did she want? Why was she here, to torture him? Maybe it was about the divorce. Maybe she wanted to hand him the signed papers in person, but she could have done that at the door instead of dragging this out.

When he walked back into the living room, she wasn't there. Had she left? She couldn't have. He hadn't heard the door. "Annie?" he called out as he strode through the dining room and saw her standing in the kitchen, looking out the window. "Are you all right?" he asked. He didn't know why she was here, but she seemed so conflicted. Was this what he had done to her?

She turned around then, and he didn't know what to say. Her coat was open, and it took him a second to register what he was looking at as she glanced down at her rounded belly and placed both hands over the cotton T-shirt that covered her baby bump. He felt as if his mouth had dried out, and he couldn't even get a breath to speak.

"I'm sorry, Sean," she said as she stood there, her hands

protectively covering the baby she was carrying. Even though he could tell she was pregnant, it was a small bump on her tiny frame.

"What?" He gestured toward her. "You're pregnant. Why didn't you tell me?"

She appeared embarrassed for a minute, and she glanced away. Maybe it wasn't even his. His expression must have shown what he was thinking as he went to walk away.

"Sean, wait." She reached for his arm. "Whatever you're thinking, I couldn't tell you."

He pulled his arm away. "I get it, you've moved on with some guy." He ran his hand over his head.

"No! Is that what you thought?" She appeared genuinely hurt. "You think I could move on just like that?" She sounded lost. "Maybe this was a mistake, coming here."

"Whoa, wait." He stepped in front of her when she made a move to leave, and she stepped back, which had Sean holding up his hands to calm her. "I'm not going to hurt you."

She swallowed. "I know that," she said, but she didn't sound sure.

"Is this my baby?"

"Yeah," she said so softly.

"And you're just getting around to telling me now?" He swore under his breath, squeezing his fists as he turned away.

"Sean, wait, where are you going?"

He turned back to her in the doorway and just stared at her, taking in how thin she appeared. It had been so long since they were together that he'd lost count of the days. "How far along?" He gestured at her as he swallowed.

"Thirty weeks."

So it had been thirty weeks since they were together. It was a lifetime, almost another tour, but they were both in the same county, within a few miles of each other. He knew where she was, when she was home. How many nights had he spent parked outside her apartment, watching, to make sure she was okay? But he'd never seen it, never seen her close enough to even notice she was pregnant. "You're barely showing. You're not eating enough."

That brought a smile out of her. It was faint, and it didn't light up her face the way her smiles always did.

"So why didn't you tell me you were pregnant?" he said. Then he had to wonder whether Zac knew. He shut his eyes and shook his head. Of course he did. How could he have kept this from him? When she didn't say anything again, he realized why she hadn't told him. "You're still scared of me. You think I'd hurt the baby. Don't answer that." He didn't really want her to tell him. It still hurt, reliving the fear he had seen in her face. He didn't ever want to see it again.

"Sean, whatever I thought before, it doesn't really matter now. Things have changed."

He stepped toward her, half expecting her to back away from him, afraid, but this time she just stood there until he stopped right in front of her. He could smell her. Her scent, it was in him. With the love he had for her, her touch, her smile, and how she smelled…he just knew she belonged to him. But she didn't anymore.

"I filed for divorce," he said. "I saw a lawyer."

"I know. I got the papers and your checks, the money you keep sending through Zac." She reached into her purse and pulled out an envelope with a confidence he hadn't seen in a while. "I didn't sign it, Sean. Tell me, do I tear it up?"

He couldn't believe she was asking him. He was giving her an out, her very own "Get away from Sean forever" card. "Are you still scared of me?" he asked. He had to know, because if she was saying what he thought she was, he didn't think he'd survive if she ran again. To have someone he loved so terrified of him that she cowered and hid and ran was worse than anything he'd seen or done in the military. He couldn't and wouldn't go through that again, not with Annie.

"I'll tell you what I am scared of: It's walking away from

you and missing the chance that we can fix this. I don't want to wake up five years from now and realize that you've worked so hard to fix yourself and I tossed it all away because I didn't have the courage to believe in you." She lifted her hand to touch his chest and then squeezed her fist hesitantly as if she was afraid to touch him. Then she took a breath and let it out as she pressed the flat of her hand to his heart before dragging her gaze slowly up to his. "I love you, Sean Robert Green."

CHAPTER 25

He was sleeping beside her, her husband, breathing in and out so softly, evenly, as he slept. She wanted to touch the curl of his hair that dragged over the tips of his ears. It was longer than it had ever been. Ever since she'd known Sean, he'd always had the same short cut. But, as with everything, things had changed.

Zac had been right. It was time to go home. It was time to give Sean a chance and let him show her that he wasn't the same. Maybe Zac was right that it had taken Annie leaving for Sean to do everything in his power to change what had happened and who he was as a result of his one bad decision.

Sean was working it through, facing his fears, facing what he'd done, living with the realization that he was responsible for the death of two of his team members. Zac had told her, and she knew he had broken Sean's confidence and spoken of something he shouldn't have. She would never tell Sean she knew, because she was starting to understand now what had driven him over the edge. And with that came the realization of how hard he had fought to come back for her.

Even though he had set her free, thinking always of what was best for her, she had only now learned from Zac how far

Sean had actually come. Even his own doctor had been encouraging him to reach out to Annie. When she asked Zac if he thought Sean could drown in a nightmare and end up on top of her, trying to squeeze the life out of her again, he'd hesitated.

She remembered his expression and what had passed between him and Diane. It was Diane who'd rested her hand on Zac's shoulder, standing behind him as he sat on the stool across from Annie, and said, "There's always a chance something could happen, Annie, because Sean is human. But he's come to terms with what he did. He's not a man over the edge. He's not fighting the battle he was. He's come to terms with that, is working through his guilt, and he's dealing with it now. He's starting to heal. Sean's not the same as he was."

Listening to Diane, just being with the two people who had protected her and been there for her from the moment she stepped off a small plane in Port Angeles, was the catalyst she needed. Was she scared? Absolutely, from that first moment she'd knocked on the door. But when Sean opened it, she'd just had to look in his eyes to see the difference. Lying here now with her husband, feeling their baby bump between them, she wasn't afraid. She had torn up the divorce papers.

Because Sean, the man she married, the man she loved, had come back to her.

ZAC & DIANE

CHAPTER 26

Whoever was at the door was leaning on the doorbell, and as far as Zac was concerned, they'd better have a damn good excuse. "I'm coming!" he called out as he finished pouring his coffee, knowing Diane was trying to sleep.

As he pulled open the door, a fist connected with his face and had him stumbling back. He felt his hot coffee splash his chest and the floor, and the mug shattered against the wall.

"What the fuck?" He landed on the ground and jumped back on his feet, staring at Sean, who was in the doorway with a smug expression.

"Sean, what are you doing?" Annie cried. "Did you hit him?" She was behind her husband, her hand on his arm. Both were dressed in sweats and hoodies as if they were getting ready to go for a run.

"Why in the hell did you hit me?" Zac said.

"Hit you? Who hit you? What's going on here?" Now Diane was there in her pajamas, her housecoat pulled on but open over her large pregnant belly. "Did you spill your coffee, Zac?"

"You didn't think you had that coming?" Sean put his hand on the small of Annie's back before guiding her inside.

She, of course, appeared a little bothered by what Sean had done.

"Sean, you didn't have to hit him," she said, wincing when she took in Zac's face.

He tasted blood where Sean's fist had connected with his jaw, and his lip was swelling.

"Sorry, Zac," Annie said. "Sean is still a little upset about the baby. I told him you wanted me to tell him."

"You should have told me, Zac," Sean said. Zac wasn't sure if he was going to hit him again. He reached around to move Diane back, but Diane, far from being a doting wife, just shook her head, taking in Sean and Zac and one of her shattered mugs on the floor, before turning and waddling into the kitchen.

"Do you feel better?" Zac asked.

Sean didn't appear to have any regrets, and at the same time he seemed almost satisfied. "No, but it helped," he said.

Zac could see clearly in Sean's expression that he was still pissed at him. "No matter how much I wanted to tell you, Sean, I'm sorry I couldn't." It really wasn't an excuse, because the fact was that the weeks of keeping Annie's secret had weighed heavily on Zac. If their roles were reversed, he'd have without a doubt seriously hurt Sean for not telling him.

"Sean, I asked Zac and Diane not to say anything," Annie added softly. "In case it helps, he didn't agree with me." She rested her hands over the baby she carried, looking up at Sean in a way Zac hadn't seen before. There was a closeness there he'd hoped they'd reach. He hoped it would last.

Sean stepped closer to Annie, right up to her, Zac now forgotten, and touched her face—a man clearly in love with his wife. "It wasn't right, Annie. I told you I deserved to know, but this is between me and Zac. As a friend, he shouldn't have kept something of this magnitude from me." He was so tender, the way he touched Annie, and she responded to him as would any woman in love. He leaned in and kissed her.

"Annie, leave those two to work it out," Diane said as she appeared in the doorway of the kitchen, holding a kettle. "Do you want some tea?" She had lines around her eyes, and she looked so tired.

"Sure." Annie shrugged and offered Zac a sympathetic glance as she started his way. Sean stepped around the broken mug behind his wife, running his hand over her lower back.

"Zac, put some ice on that before it's the size of a baseball," Diane called out from the kitchen. She wasn't the type of woman who was going to fuss over him, but she did reach into the freezer for a bag of frozen peas as Zac tossed the pieces of the broken mug in the garbage along with the paper towel he'd used to wipe up the coffee.

He turned just as Diane tossed the bag of peas his way. He caught it one handed and pressed it to his lip, but the sting had him wincing as he took in Sean standing protectively over Annie.

"I take it"—Diane gestured towards them as she filled up the kettle with water—"that there's been some progress between you two?" She plugged the kettle in and shuffled over to the table to sit down across from Annie. She was moving slower, he had noticed over the past few days. She struggled with getting up, and she wasn't sleeping well, waking several times in the night. She had a heaviness in her eyes that hadn't been there before.

Annie smiled as she glanced up to Sean, who was hovering rather close to her. "Yeah, you could say we've worked through a lot. I'm not ready to throw in the towel—and thank you, Zac and Diane, for your gentle nudge for me to reach out to Sean. I'm so glad I did. See, Sean? You should be thanking Zac instead of hitting him."

Zac walked behind the counter, eyeing Sean, wondering

whether his friend was about to lose it again. He apparently didn't agree with Annie.

"Just wondering, was that your way of thanking me, too?" Zac said, and Sean just shrugged.

"Sean." Annie nudged him. "Remember you wanted to ask Zac about…" She was sounding mysterious.

"Ask me what?"

Diane seemed just as curious as he was, as she watched them as the kettle boiled. She started to get up, but Zac waved her back down. "What herbal stuff do you want this morning?" he asked, rummaging in the cupboard for the box of herbal teas. Diane had finally given in and started drinking them a few months ago after Zac nagged her to stop with the coffee.

"The apple cinnamon," she said. "It's the only one that's somewhat drinkable."

He had to smile at that, since she'd been a trooper with just about everything about this pregnancy, especially considering she was the one who'd had to adjust her entire lifestyle for him.

"Annie?" Zac gestured with the box as he grabbed two mugs, dumping a tea bag in one.

"Ooh, lemon if you have it."

"Lemon it is." He poured boiling water into both mugs. "So what's up? What do you want to ask?"

Sean had now crossed his arms over his chest. "I need a hand packing up Annie's apartment and bringing everything back home again."

"Well, I can pack it up, Sean. I told you," Annie said as Zac set two steaming mugs in front of her and Diane.

"No, Zac can help me," Sean said. "You can stay home and rest, take it easy. You've done enough already this morning, insisting on going for a run."

So that was why they were dressed that way.

"You didn't let me run, though," Annie said. "We only did

half a mile."

"You did run. You're supposed to be taking it easy, and I let you jog. You're not training for a marathon." Sean appeared ready to argue with her.

"Moving sounds great," Zac said, jumping in before Sean could say something else that would put him in the doghouse with Annie. "Sure I can help. That's great about you moving back, Annie." He winked at her. "What about your job?"

"I'm keeping it," she said at the same time that Sean said, "She's quitting."

"Annie," Sean said, "I'm not kidding. Look at you. You're so thin, and you haven't been looking after yourself. It's time for me to look after you, so let me."

He was being pigheaded, and for a moment Zac wanted to pull him aside and tell him to cool it, but he said, "Sean's right, Annie. You've had Diane and me worried." He wanted to add a lot more, because they'd both noticed how thin Annie had been for how far along she was in her pregnancy. Zac had even mentioned the possibility of her tagging along on one of Diane's doctor's appointments just the night before.

Diane slid back her chair and struggled to get up, shaking her head as she strode past Zac, her hand on her lower back. "It sounds as if you two still have a lot to work out, logistics wise. I'm going to grab a shower." She stopped in the doorway and glanced back at them. Annie was shaking her head as if getting ready to argue. "Annie, take my advice as one pregnant woman to another. Let Sean hover. Take it easy. You need to look after you and that baby first right now."

"But we're fine, we're good," she said. Maybe it was the way she said it that had Zac wondering whether there was more. But then, maybe he was reading into it too much, considering the emotional roller coaster Annie and Sean had been on. This was new, and she was probably still trying to find her footing in rebuilding a life with Sean.

"So when do you want my help to move Annie's things?" Zac said.

Sean was looking down at Annie. Obviously, he too knew something was up with his wife. "Since you and I are both off today, I was thinking now," he said. "Let's get all her things back home this morning if you can. Otherwise, it'll have to wait a few days, and then I know Annie will decide she needs some things and she'll start moving everything herself."

Before Zac could say anything, Diane started back into the kitchen. "Great idea," she said. "Why don't you two go do that now? Annie can stay here."

Sean seemed pleased. "Sounds like a plan," he said. He leaned down and kissed Annie before starting out of the kitchen, and when Zac looked over at his wife and then back at Annie, who was now frowning, he realized that Diane planned on having a heart-to-heart with Annie, getting to the bottom of whatever this was she appeared to still be holding on to.

He leaned in and kissed Diane. "You take it easy until I get back."

She just rolled her eyes, which was so unlike her—but he also knew she was going stir crazy. Well, he'd see what he could do for her when he got back.

CHAPTER 27

Diane felt a little better after showering and dressing in a pair of cotton maternity pants and a very comfortable light shirt. The outfit matched her mood, gray and frumpy, and was at least baggy enough that it provided some comfort even though her back hadn't stopped aching in weeks. "They're long gone, so do you mind telling me what's really going on with you?" she said.

Annie was sitting in the living room with her feet up on the ottoman and a steaming mug in her hands. She didn't say anything for a minute as she suddenly went quiet, glancing down at her hot tea before taking another sip.

Diane was usually so patient, but she had been starting to go a little stir crazy since hanging up her badge the other day. Being home all day, she was beginning to feel the walls closing in, and having Annie sitting there, holding on to whatever this was…well, she was wearing on Diane's patience. So Diane picked up a cushion and tossed it at Annie's foot.

"Come on, out with it," she said. "Don't think I didn't miss whatever that hesitation was. Especially after what you and Sean have been through together, I have a hard time believing that after one day, everything is just peachy. If you recall, you were sitting in that very same spot less than twenty-four hours ago. Sean had served you with divorce papers, and Zac and I were having a heart-to-heart with you about the realities of where Sean was—is, pardon me."

Annie was now biting her lip and glancing down at her mug again as if she'd been caught in a lie and didn't know how to respond. "Okay, fine. Maybe we're really good, and last night I had the best sleep beside my husband since before all this, without the worry that something would happen with Sean and he'd snap. It was something I realized I had been holding on to this morning, and it was gone. Sean has changed. He's really worked hard to bring himself back, and for a time, even waking up this morning in his arms, I thought we were back to Annie and Sean before all this happened."

"And you're worried about…?" Diane was having to prod her along.

"This is all so new—and it's good, and maybe I had all but given up hope for Sean and me, that I'd ever feel safe around him again, but there's also the memory of that night so long ago that put that fear in me. I was afraid I would never again feel safe with him, and I did last night, and today, I mean, you saw." She gestured vaguely.

Diane could see how Annie was contemplating a lot. "Don't overthink, Annie. Sean is right about a few things, and Zac has noticed, as well. You need to take it easy, and I for one am probably the last person to give the advice that taking time off work is a good idea so you can take care of you and that baby, but it is a good idea. And another thing: you are way too skinny."

Annie frowned at that and then shrugged. "I haven't had much of an appetite. You know it's hard to eat when your heart is in your throat."

"But it isn't anymore," Diane said, "and you do need to

eat for the baby. I mean, what has your doctor said? I know mine has been all over my weight gain, which he says has been too much the past six weeks, but then, with Zac shoving food my way every time I turn around, it's a wonder I'm not three hundred pounds."

Annie had an odd look on her face.

"Annie, you're making me a little nervous. What the hell is it with you, girl? What did your doctor say?"

She shrugged. "I haven't seen anyone yet."

Diane wasn't sure whether her shock registered on her face. For the first time in her life, she couldn't even form one intelligent word. She breathed out, her mouth open, and Annie bit down on a piece of her thumbnail and then winced.

"I know you probably want to call me an idiot, and there's no excuse," she said.

"Yeah, you're right. I do want to call you an idiot, for a lot of reasons, but this is something I see with those on the streets —starving, poor, drug users. Take your pick, but you aren't any of them. What the hell were you thinking, Annie? You don't mess around with proper prenatal care. You're pregnant. Prenatal care is an absolute must. What the hell are you doing?" Diane slapped her hand into her palm to drive the point home. "I know you're not a stupid person, so tell me why you never said a thing about not seeing a doctor? Oh my good God, when I tell Zac, he's going to freak and wonder why you didn't say something to us—to me. Why?" She jammed her hands in her hair, realizing Sean was going to be furious, and rightly so.

"It's not what you think, Diane."

"You don't know what I'm thinking, but a whole bunch of things are going through my mind. Could you not find a doctor, or...?" Diane held up her hands. Why hadn't Annie asked for the name of her doctor if she was having trouble? Why hadn't Diane taken her in hand and given her a name anyway?

"I called a doctor close to where I work," Annie said. "It's just that the first time, they had an emergency and had to reschedule, and then I had to cancel, as my boss needed a proposal done up for a new tour operator. I had to stay late, and then I found out from human resources that my health care wasn't going to be in effect for another month, so I kind of waited."

"Healthcare, this is about healthcare?" Diane said. Had Sean left her to fend for herself? He hadn't known she was pregnant. "Weren't you under Sean's?"

"Sean has great healthcare, and I was, but I didn't feel right using it since we weren't together, and he didn't know about the baby. I didn't want it getting back to him, so I waited and told myself it would be okay. It was just another month, I told myself. It was just because it was a new job, and I didn't have coverage the first six months. But it should be in force now, and I planned this week to call to make the appointment and get in there and see him."

"Okay, Annie, you need to tell Sean. You need to call this doctor and get in to see him today. If he won't see you, you call mine. Better yet"—Diane pulled out a scratch pad and pen from the end table beside her and scribbled down her doctor's number—"call the doctor now, or I'll call Zac, and he will tell Sean this time." She ripped the paper and held it out to Annie, who scooted out of her chair and took it. "Seriously, Annie, call now. This isn't something to mess around with."

"I know that, and thank you." She held up the paper. "I'll call my doctor first."

Diane pointed to the phone on the hall table. Annie just rolled her eyes as she strode over to it, picked it up, and started dialing as she walked into the other room.

Sean would be pretty pissed about this, and since he hadn't known Annie was pregnant and Zac had, he'd likely throw another punch her husband's way. What had she been thinking?

"Okay, you can stop worrying now," Annie said. "My doctor can fit me in in the next thirty minutes or I'll have to wait until next week. The only problem is I don't have my car. Sean drove."

Diane could do one of two things: give Annie her car keys and let her drive, or pull herself off the sofa and take Annie herself even though she'd promised Zac she'd take it easy. It was only driving. She could do that much.

Diane struggled to her feet. "Let's go. At least we'll save Zac from having your husband's fist in his face again."

"I'm so sorry, Diane. I never expected Sean to do that," Annie said, but the amusement in her face told a different story. "This may sound weird, but in an odd way, what Sean did made me feel loved."

What was it about these alpha males who tended to lead with their fists instead of their brains? Diane would be the last person to agree with Annie, even though having a man fight for her touched her in a way she'd never acknowledge to anyone. Zac had and would always have her back. If she had to trade that in for someone who reasoned and sat back and let things happen, she honestly didn't think she'd be truly happy. No, there was something about the difficult man in her life that added a depth of complexity to their relationship.

She said the only thing she could think of as she reached for her keys and jacket: "Well, let's go, then, and not give Sean another reason to show you how much he loves you."

CHAPTER 28

Zac didn't miss the way Sean took in the tiny one-bedroom apartment Annie had lived in. It really was plain, nothing special, with concrete block walls painted white, tweed furniture from the eighties, and pressboard tables and dressers, bargain basement and cheap. It was clean, though, and Zac knew it was what Annie could afford comfortably. As Annie had said repeatedly to both him and Diane, it was close to work, and it was a roof over her head, which had been all she needed.

Sean tossed the boxes he'd picked up from a local supermarket on the floor. "Well, let's pack everything up and get the hell out of here." He was shaking his head as walked into the bedroom and then the bath. "She really didn't have much with her."

"She did the best she could, Sean. Does it really matter now?" Zac hoped he wouldn't bring it up with Annie, not now.

Sean pulled open the fridge and then the cupboards. "I guess not, considering she's got very little food here, either. Did you see how thin she was? I mean, Annie's always had a great figure, but she's too skinny right now. I can see she wasn't doing much cooking. There's a box of cereal, some crackers, a box of tea, and a small piece of cheese and some milk in the fridge." Sean pulled out the cottage cheese container, opened it, made a face, and dumped it in the sink. "Rotten," he said, appearing annoyed.

Zac started to wonder why he had missed this. He should have picked up on the fact that Annie didn't appear to be eating, but it made no sense. He had been bringing her money from Sean, so he knew she'd had enough.

Sean started pulling open drawers, Zac didn't know what he was looking for, but he could hear him in the bedroom as Zac put the boxes he was carrying on the table.

A wad of cash landed on the table next to them. "I guess she decided not to use the money," Sean said, irritated, gesturing at the cash. "So she's been working a job that pays little more than minimum wage, and she prefers to starve herself instead of using the money I sent. Explain that to me so I can understand, because it's looking to me like she didn't care enough about the baby, my baby, let alone herself."

"Whoa, stop there, Sean. Before you go any further down that path, you need to talk to Annie about this. There could be way more than we know." She was heartbroken, more than she'd let on. That much was certain. "She's back home with you, so don't create a problem before you know for sure." He knew that sounded reasonable, and he was also aware that if this had been Diane, all hell would have broken loose. But then, Diane wasn't one to starve herself.

Sean was shaking his head as he grabbed a box, then picked up the wad of cash and stuffed it in his pocket. "What's there to explain, Zac? I haven't seen her in months, or I would have noticed. Why didn't you?"

Well, there was the accusation he'd expected. He had noticed, even said something to Diane, and they'd had her over and visited regularly. He'd just never expected this. There had to be an explanation, a reasonable one. As he watched Sean and the accusation staring back at him, he realized he'd been wrong on a lot of fronts. "Can we just agree that now you've got Annie back, you can stay on top of looking after her and the baby? All I know, Sean, is that Annie was pretty torn up about not having you. She tried to hide it, but we noticed her puffy eyes, how she would cry."

Maybe he should have done more, but short of packing Annie up and moving her back in with him and Diane, he wasn't sure how else he could have watched over her. "We came by often. I know we pushed her, asked if she was okay, helped where she'd let us, but your wife is independent, maybe too much for her own good."

Sean grunted. "I'd say yours is the same."

He was right about that, but at least Diane had listened and was at home with her feet up, taking it easy these last few weeks until the baby was due. He'd won that argument, although not by much.

Sean lifted a box. "I'll pack up the bedroom and bath. How about you pack up everything in the kitchen, whatever's hers, and then I'd like to get out of here, go and collect my wife, and sit her down and have a long talk with her—starting with the fact that from this day forward, her only consideration is looking after herself and the baby. And, by God, she will eat."

Zac wondered whether his expression showed his surprise at Sean, at how far he'd come from pushing Annie away to doing everything he could to look after her. It made Zac proud.

"What?" Sean asked.

Zac just shook his head. "Nothing. Go so we can get out of here. I have my own wife at home I'd like to check on."

As Zac emptied the bare cupboards of the few items Annie

had, he stopped for just a minute, thankful he had a wife like Diane. She was so strong, independent, and his. Even though she had fought him tooth and nail, he realized deep down that all she wanted was to be loved—and he did very much love her.

CHAPTER 29

Zac had called Diane twice and left a message, and he now checked his cell phone again because she hadn't called him back. That was unlike her. He'd have panicked long ago if Annie hadn't been at home with her.

Sean closed up the back of his truck. Since Annie didn't have much, they hadn't needed a second vehicle. "Any answer?" he asked as he climbed in the driver's side.

"No. I left another message. Maybe they went out for a walk," Zac said, but then, he'd called Diane's cell, too, and she never left home without it. It too had gone to voicemail.

Sean started his pickup and dialed his phone left handed. He was shaking his head. "Annie, it's Sean. Where the hell are you and Diane, and why aren't you answering the phone?" He hung up.

"You know what? I'm not liking this, any of it," Zac said as Sean drove. "Do you think you can punch it in gear? Let's get back to my place and find out what's going on."

It was a short drive out, even though the fifteen minutes seemed like an eternity. Zac found himself fearing the worst. With Diane, those fears were something he'd had to figure out a way to contain. Even though he dealt with his old scars the best he could, they always lingered in the back of his mind. Something could have happened to her and the baby.

"Looks like Diane's four by four is gone," Sean said as he parked. Zac tried to figure out why Diane hadn't called him and let him know they were going out. She was good about calling him.

"Maybe they went back to our place," Sean said as he parked behind Zac's truck, and Zac could tell that Sean wanted to head back to his house and check.

"Without calling and letting either of us know?" Zac said as he pulled open the passenger door and climbed out. He could hear Sean behind him, his boots crunching through the gravel. Zac was through the front door and flicking on the lights in the late afternoon dimness. For a moment, he just stood there, taking in the house as he would a crime scene.

He didn't know why he did that at times, but it was his way of gathering information objectively before his emotions could cloud his reasoning. There was a mug on the end table, the tag of a teabag dangling out. A pillow lay on the floor by the sofa. The kitchen was neat and tidy except for a plate with crumbs and half an apple cut up on the cutting board. Nothing was off.

"What's wrong?" Sean must have been watching him as he stood in the doorway, looking around.

Zac did what he always did when people tried to get into his head, when he let his guard down enough that someone could wonder what he was thinking. He shook his head. "Nothing. That's the problem." He wandered to the counter and then over to the table to find the phone sitting there, but there was no note. He picked up the phone and pressed the buttons, maneuvering through the call list. Who had she called last? Obviously not her husband to let him know she was going out.

It was a doctor, but not hers. He pressed the button and called the number. He could feel Sean behind him, watching.

"What's going on, Zac?"

"Don't know yet. She called some doctor in Sequim," he said. "Why would you do that, Diane?"

"Doctor Fletcher," a female voice answered.

"I'm wondering if you can tell me whether my wife, Diane Zacorbosky, was in earlier today?"

"I'm sorry, sir. I can't give out patient information."

He didn't like being jerked around, and this receptionist was poking a cornered lion. That just wasn't smart. "Listen, I'm not asking for patient information, I'm just asking about my wife. She's thirty-six weeks pregnant. Her doctor is Doctor Blaseck in Port Townsend."

"I don't have a patient by that name," she said.

Zac shut his eyes, wondering whether Diane was still using her maiden name. They had argued when she refused to take his, but they'd eventually agreed that she'd keep hers for work and take his for all legal records. "How about under Diane Larsen?" He was sure he'd spit out the name, praying she wasn't using it.

There was a hesitation on the other end. "Sir?"

"My wife's maiden name, although I don't know why she'd use it, not for this."

"No, I'm afraid not," the woman said.

"Zac, what about Annie?" Sean was right in front of him. Why hadn't he thought of Annie?

"What about Annie Green?"

The woman sighed. "Another of your wife's names?"

"No, her friend who's also pregnant and was here with her today."

"I did have a call from Annie Green."

Zac slipped the receiver away from his mouth. "You're right, it was Annie."

"But she didn't arrive at her appointment again," the woman said.

"I'm sorry, what do you mean? How long ago was her

appointment?" Now Zac was starting to have a full-fledged panic attack, his head going to all those places he'd tried to keep himself away from.

"Her appointment was at ten thirty," she said. It was almost four. Definitely time to worry.

"And you said she's missed other appointments?"

The woman hesitated on the other end. "Sir, Annie Green has never met the doctor."

As Zac set down the disconnected phone on the table, he glanced up at Sean, who had obviously heard what the nurse said.

"What the hell is going on, Zac?" he said. Then he stopped himself from asking any more questions. "You know what? Right now I would love to give my lovely wife a shake and ask her what the fuck she's thinking, but I just got her back, and there's a whole bunch about what I'm learning today that I'm not liking."

Zac held up his hand to shut Sean up. "Shh," he said, doing his best to take a breath and ground himself before he did the one thing he wanted to do right now: race out the door and start looking for Diane. He called her cell phone again, and it kicked him right to voicemail.

"Right now, I'll be right beside you, and I'll sit my wife down right beside yours, but first we need to find them. With the fact that Annie was supposed to be at a doctor's appointment and didn't show, and no one is answering, I'm getting a really bad feeling. Where the hell are they?"

"Does Diane have a habit of taking off and disappearing?" Sean had pulled out his cell phone.

"No, she doesn't. She's about as levelheaded as they come. You call the hospital, both of them, the ones in Port Angeles and Port Townsend."

Sean was already dialing. "And who are you calling?"

Zac had the phone to his ear. "Diane's precinct."

Sean only nodded as he turned away, talking into the phone.

Zac made his own call to Diane's sergeant and boss, who was probably the last person she'd want him to call. But right now, Zac would call in the entire army if that would help him find his wife.

CHAPTER 30

Diane's head felt as if she'd rammed it through a brick wall. She wanted to say something, ask for something, but the thought of opening her mouth to speak was the equivalent of someone slamming a hammer to her head over and over. Then the hammer was in her ribs, her chest, and she felt an incredible pressure in her stomach and lower. She was leaning at an odd angle.

"Diane…"

She heard her name called from a distance. It hurt to think, but slowly she realized something wasn't right.

"Diane, please."

She heard the voice again: Annie. She tried to talk, but all she could get out was a sound. What was wrong with her? There was ringing again. It was familiar, but it seemed so far away.

"Diane, I can't get out." It was Annie, and she sounded scared, but Diane was so tired.

She blinked, forcing her eyes to open, but good grief, did it hurt. It was horrible, the pain shooting out from her head. Then she realized her cheek was pressed to something hard, the steering wheel. What had happened? She wasn't sure whether she had said it out loud. No, she hadn't. Her mouth hadn't moved. It hurt too much.

It took a minute for her to understand what she was seeing, as there was steam—or was that smoke?—and glass. She could feel it on her now. There was a tree or branch right in front of her. No wonder she couldn't see Annie.

"Annie?" Her voice sounded so odd, and she swallowed. "I can't see you." She reached up and touched the branch right beside her, coming through the middle of the vehicle. She could hear a hiss.

"You hit a tree," Annie said. "It came through the windshield. I'm here, I just can't get out."

Diane tried to lift her head and then stopped. "I hit a tree. How'd I hit a tree? The airbag didn't go off. What happened?" She couldn't remember anything. They had been driving along the highway, and she had been talking to Annie. The doctor, they had been going to see the doctor.

"Diane, you passed out. We were talking, and you just fell forward over the steering wheel and drove us over the embankment. I tried to grab the wheel, but your foot was on the gas, and we drove right into the trees. One came right through the windshield, between us. I was so scared you were dead. You didn't answer for so long." Annie's voice was high pitched and shaking. Diane knew the sound of shock.

"How long was I out?" How could she have passed out behind the wheel? She'd never so much as fainted. Oh no, the baby! She could have killed them.

"I don't know," Annie said.

"Annie, your cell phone. Can you reach it?" Diane slid her hand over the branch that seemed to fill the middle of the vehicle. She loved trees, but not now. She tried to feel for her cell phone, which she always tucked in the center cup holder, but she could only feel something sharp and jagged pressed up against her leg.

"It's in my purse, behind my seat in back," Annie said. "I can't reach it. I tried already."

This wasn't good, as Diane could feel wetness between her legs and a sharp pain low in her back, then a sharpness in her groin that took her breath away. She could hear Annie saying something as she fought through the excruciating tearing in her thighs, and she could do nothing. It seemed to go on forever and then slowly eased. She knew then that they were in trouble.

"Annie, I think my water broke. I'm wet. I'm pretty sure I'm in labor." Her arm was pressed to the door, and she slid her hand over the handle. She grabbed hold and pulled, but nothing happened. "The door's stuck. Annie, can you get out your door?"

"I've been trying. I cracked it open, but the door's wedged against a tree."

The phone was ringing again. She could hear it. "Annie, that's my phone. Can you see it?" She needed to get that phone. She pulled at the door handle again.

"Oh, my leg is stuck!" Annie said. "I can't turn." Then she cried out in pain, but there was nothing Diane could do, as she was fighting through her own hell. She wished Zac were there. She hadn't even called him to tell him where she was going.

"I think my leg is broken, Diane. I can't move. It's pinned under the dash. Help!" she screamed.

All Diane could do was ride the wave of pain and pray that someone had seen them drive off the road and already called for help.

CHAPTER 31

The good news was that Annie and Diane weren't at the hospital. Sean had called both Port Angeles and Port Townsend, and no pregnant women had come into the emergency room. Green, Diane's sergeant, had put out an alert on Diane's vehicle. They'd already checked to see if there were any accident reports, and nothing had come in, which was good news. Of course, the only problem was that Diane still wasn't answering her phone. Annie hadn't shown up for her doctor's appointment, and her cell phone kept going to voicemail. It was as if both women had dropped off the face of the earth.

Green had suggested that Diane may have gone shopping or out to lunch with friends and turned off her phone, and he had implied Zac should stop being an overprotective husband. The problem with that scenario was that Diane wasn't the kind of woman who spent a few hours shopping and then going out for lunch, shutting off her phone and not answering for hours. Added to that was the timeline Zac had built: Diane had been driving Annie to the doctor for whatever reason—none of which he liked—and neither had arrived.

"I don't care if you have to call the national guard. I want my wife found. This is Diane we're talking about. You've worked with her a lot of years. Do you really believe she's the type of woman who just goes off?"

There was rustling on the other end. Green could be a real prick sometimes, especially where Diane was concerned. "Look, my hands are tied. Dispatch has already alerted units to keep an eye out for Diane, and I'm sure she's going to feel embarrassed having everyone in this county looking for her. Just give it a few more hours, and then if she doesn't show, we can launch a search."

Zac wasn't waiting, though. There was no way in hell. "She has her cell phone on her. Here's the number. Use the GPS on the phone to locate her. I'm not asking, Green. I'm telling you, find my wife or I swear I'll go above your head. You really want to piss me off? If something has happened to Diane and you don't help me out, I swear to God I'll bring holy hell down upon you. You don't want a war with me."

Even Sean gave him an odd look, but at the same time he was pacing the living room and stopping at the door, pulling it open and looking out every few minutes.

"Fine. It'll take a few minutes," Green said.

"No longer. I'm heading out and driving toward Sequim. You call my cell phone when you find out something." Zac pulled on his black coat. It was cooler now in the afternoons, and even colder at night. He slipped his cell phone in his pocket.

"Ready?" Sean said, pulling his keys from his pocket.

"Maybe I should follow behind you," Zac suggested. Taking two vehicles would let them cover more area.

Sean was out the door and down the steps. "Up to you, but I think two sets of eyes in one vehicle would be better. I just want to start looking either way." Sean opened his driver's door, and Zac followed, stopping in front of his truck. Then he looked over to Sean, who rolled down his window just as Zac's cell phone rang.

He saw it was Green calling back. "That was quick. What did you find out?"

"I just sent you a text of the location. About five miles outside of Sequim, past Blyn. I've sent a unit out that way because there's nothing around there, just highway and trees."

"Great, on my way." Zac pocketed his phone. "You drive," he said as he climbed in the passenger side of Sean's car, realizing Green wasn't so bad after all.

CHAPTER 32

"I can reach it, just. My fingers are on it!" Annie called out. "Diane, my leg is bleeding really bad. I don't feel so good."

Diane had been struggling with the door. She'd managed to unfasten her seatbelt, but the door was jammed. It wasn't opening. "I know, Annie, but we have to get out of here and at least call for help. I'm pinned where I am, and I'll be dammed if I have my baby here. Zac is going to kill me." Worse than that, she knew how badly this would hurt him. She had to get out of there—get them both out of there.

"I got it!" Annie called. "Oh, shit, I dropped it."

Diane shut her eyes in defeat as she heard Annie struggling, reaching around the seat. "How far off the road are we? Did no one see us?" She couldn't believe that no one had seen them leave the road at this time of day, yet no one was there trying to help them.

"I think we're pretty far off. We were going fast when we hit. We're in the trees, so probably not easily seen. Oh, oh, I think I got it."

"Don't drop it this time. You can do it." Diane pleaded in her head for Annie to get her phone. They needed to call Zac.

He'd be beside himself. All the ringing had to have been him calling over and over. She knew Zac. He'd been checking up on her more and more as of late.

"I got it. Diane, the battery is almost dead," Annie said.

"Call Zac. He's the first number."

She could hear rustling again, but she couldn't see Annie at all.

"It's ringing," she heard Annie say. "Zac, Zac, it's Annie!"

"Tell him where we are!" she yelled. "Zac, it's Diane!"

She could hear Annie crying and talking. She was sure she could hear Zac yelling, but she was struggling for breath. The pain had come out of nowhere. At least Zac knew, and he'd come. He'd find her. She leaned against the door in relief and yelled when the pain became too much.

Zac's phone rang just as Sean drove around the corner of the highway. A deputy's cruiser was parked on the side of the road.

"Stop here!" Zac said, pointing, and Sean pulled off the shoulder and parked behind the cruiser. Zac saw Diane's name on his screen. "Diane, where the hell are you? I've got half the county out looking—"

"Zac, Zac, it's Annie!" She sounded panicked.

"Annie, where are you? Are you all right?" He opened his door, and Sean was practically all over him, reaching out to grab for the cell phone.

"Where's Annie? Let me talk to her," Sean demanded.

Zac climbed out. He could hear Sean slam his door and come racing around the vehicle.

"Zac, we were in an accident. We went off the road. I don't know where, exactly, but we can't get out." She was crying and panicking, and static was cutting into the call. Then he heard Diane yelling in the background.

"They went off the road!" Zac yelled. Sean was with the deputy, following tire tracks in the grass. One of them yelled and started running.

"I see the car. Annie!" Sean cried.

Zac saw Diane's SUV down the embankment, brush around it so only the back end was sticking out. It was a moment in time that came out of nowhere and sucker punched him. For a second, he wasn't sure he could breathe.

He climbed over a log and pushed back branches, sliding around to the driver's door, and he saw her. "Diane!"

She turned her head. She had blood on her cheek. "Zac, I can't get out. My water broke," she said. Then she screamed.

"I'll call for an ambulance," the deputy called out, and Sean was around the other side, yanking on the door. Zac could hear metal grinding. The vehicle was shaking.

"Annie, where else are you hurt?" Sean called out. "Give me a hand with this door!"

The deputy had climbed over to help Sean, and Zac pulled at Diane's door, which wouldn't budge. He took in the shattered windshield, the tree coming through the front. "Diane, close your eyes," he said. "I'm going to break this glass."

She turned her face, and Zac used his sleeve to push the windshield in more. Then he pulled off his coat, reaching in and covering her to protect her from any more glass.

"Zac, I'm in labor," she cried out, panicked.

Zac slid onto the front of the vehicle and used his foot to push away the rest of the glass. He reached inside, pulling his coat down and shaking off the glass. He checked her pulse. "Where does it hurt?" he asked her as he took in the cut on her cheek and the swelling on her forehead.

She was grimacing and reached up to take his hand. She squeezed it as she screamed out.

"I'm going to get you out of here!" he yelled.

Then Annie screamed and cried, "My leg! It's stuck."

"Dammit, Annie, I need to stop the bleeding. Hold your hand there," Sean yelled.

"Sean, how's Annie?" Zac said. He didn't like what he was hearing.

There was no way he was getting Diane out except through her door, and there was no way she could deliver a baby, pinned in as she was.

"Her leg is pinned under the dash," Sean said. "There's a lot of blood. Can't tell where it's coming from."

Could this be any worse?

"EMT is three minutes away," the deputy called out, but three minutes was too long if Annie was bleeding that bad and Diane was in active labor.

"Diane, I need to check Annie," Zac said. "I'll be right back."

She let go of his hand, her head back on the seat, her eyes closed. "Go," she choked out. He could tell she was in pain, but she was playing the tough girl, the same act she'd put on for him when he met her. Unlike everyone else, though, he could see past all that bravado to her vulnerability. He also knew it was her way of protecting her heart.

"Hey, I'm not kidding, Diane. You know damn well I'll be back. Annie's bleeding."

This time, what looked back at him was a scared woman, his wife, who depended on him.

"You listen to me," he said. "I promise you I'm going to get you out of here."

She choked on a sob. Her lip quivered as a tear fell. "Okay," she said.

He squeezed her hand again and moved back off the hood of the vehicle. Because the SUV was wrapped so far around the tree, he had to climb through the brush and around the back to get to Annie's side.

Sean and the deputy had managed to get the door open, but part of the dash was pushed down onto Annie's right leg, and there was so much blood. She had a cut above her brow, and her jacket was torn.

"Annie, how're you doing?" Zac asked her. She was struggling for breath, her eyelids heavy, and he could tell she'd lost a lot of blood. "Sean, give me your belt."

"Zac, how's Diane?" Annie said. She was breathing hard. "She passed out at the wheel, and we…I couldn't wake her."

"We're going to get you both out," Zac said. He took Sean's belt and started to slip it around her thigh. "This is going to hurt, Annie, but I need to stop the bleeding." He didn't give her any time as he pulled it tight, and she screamed. "Sean, hold this!" He moved Sean in to hold the belt and her hand.

He could hear the ambulance now along with other emergency vehicles. It was about fucking time, he wanted to yell out, but he really was thankful as he listened to the sounds of the help that had just arrived.

He made it back around the vehicle just in time to see Diane slump to the side.

CHAPTER 33

She heard talking vaguely, off and on. She heard Sean's voice fade in and out and Zac's urgent demands for her to open her eyes. He was there, always there. She didn't know if she had spoken. She wanted to tell him it was okay, to stop worrying, but she also wanted to touch him. She was so tired. She kept fading in and out, and when she finally opened her eyes, her head was pounding with one of the worst headaches she'd ever had.

Then she realized the white she was looking at was the ceiling, and it took a minute of looking around to understand she was in the hospital. She raised her hand and felt it pinch from the IV taped there. She hurt so bad. It hurt to move. She hissed and sucked in a breath, hearing a rustle.

"Hey, you're awake," Zac said. He looked like crap. It looked like he hadn't shaved in a couple of days, and he had lines under his eyes as if he hadn't slept.

"The baby?" She winced because it hurt to talk, and she was so scared for a minute that her heart ached something fierce. What had she done?

"Hey, it's okay. It's a boy, six pounds. He's big for only

thirty-six weeks, but strong." The way Zac said it, she was sure there were tears in his eyes.

Maybe it was a rush of emotion or the shock, she didn't know, but she felt her throat thicken, and that made her mad, because she didn't cry. "Dammit, Zac, are you sure he's okay?" She was hurting, and she wondered whether she'd made a face, as Zac pushed the call button.

"You need something for the pain," he said.

She really did, but she didn't want to go to sleep. "I want to stay awake. I want to see him. I'm sorry," Diane said. "I couldn't get out."

"Hey, you and I are going to have a really long talk when you get out of here." He looked so serious, and she could tell there was something he was holding back. She knew him so well, her guy, her husband. Then she remembered: Annie, the accident. She'd been driving.

"Annie, is she okay? Where is she?" She tried to move, but her abdomen hurt.

"You had surgery, an emergency C-section. Your body has been through a trauma. Just relax. Annie lost a lot of blood." Zac glanced away a second, and she knew there was more, way more. She couldn't help thinking the worst, and of course she was responsible.

"Oh, Zac, no, Annie…"

He was shaking his head. "Hey, no, no. She's in ICU. She lost a lot of blood, and she went into early labor. They were aggressive to try to stop it, but because of the blood loss and trauma, they had to deliver the baby." Zac was leaning over her, his arms on both her sides. She needed to feel him as she touched his forearm, holding on to him.

The baby had to have died, and it was her fault.

"The baby is in ICU," Zac said, "about twenty-eight weeks' gestation and on a ventilator. We don't know anything else. Annie lost about twenty percent of her blood volume.

Her leg was crushed, but she had surgery, and they had to put pins in to stabilize it. She'll need physio."

"It's my fault," Diane said. "I don't know what happened. I was driving Annie to the doctor. She'd never seen a doctor for the baby, and I was so mad she hadn't been looking after herself. I don't know what happened. I heard Annie yelling."

There were so many things she wanted to ask, to share, to talk to Zac about, but she needed to see her baby. "I want to see him," she said again.

Zac was shaking his head. "You need rest," he said. He was being Zac, overprotective, and she wanted to argue, but her head hurt.

"Zac, please, I just need to see him, please," she said again, so softly.

The door opened, and Zac looked up and over. "She's awake. She needs something for the pain."

It was an older redheaded nurse who approached in pink scrubs, a stethoscope around her neck. "I'll get you something for the pain. Let me just check you first." The nurse checked her vitals and then left, closing the door behind her.

Zac was watching over her. Good grief, she loved him. He was the only man to see her vulnerability and to really know that she needed him far more than she would ever admit. He touched her face with the back of his fingers, and she held his hand. He was so strong.

"I don't want to depend on you," she said. She could feel the way he pulled back. Maybe he didn't understand. "I'm scared sometimes it'll be too much for you."

He leaned down, resting his hands again on either side of her. "Have I ever shown you I can't handle something?" He frowned, and she knew she'd made him angry.

"No, and that's what scares me. I've never allowed myself to tell anyone how scared I am. I've had to be strong, stand on my own two feet, and be careful of what I share—but you know everything about me, what scares me, everything."

Maybe he was understanding what she was saying, as he sat on the edge of the bed, touching her. "You're one damn strong lady, and you're mine. I'm not going anywhere, but what I can't handle, Diane, is you not talking to me and taking off, and then I'm worrying something has happened to you—which it did. You shouldn't have been driving. They said your blood sugar was low. They suspect you fainted. You're lucky it wasn't worse. It could have been worse!"

She knew what he was saying. She'd screwed up even though it was one of those things she'd seen a hundred times herself as a cop. "How did you get me out?" She couldn't remember a thing.

Something in his expression made him clear his throat before he could speak again. "It's amazing what you can do when you have to. You passed out. Your entire department was there—Green, too. They helped me get your door open. We got you out. You scared the hell out of me, Diane. Annie wasn't so lucky. The dash had to be cut away to get her out." He brushed back her short hair as the nurse came back in with pain meds.

"I'm sorry," she said. She swallowed the pills as Zac hovered, understanding now how scared he had been. "I still want to see the baby now."

She didn't miss the exchange between the nurse and Zac, and it was the nurse who said, "I think we can arrange that. Let me grab a wheelchair for you and I'll be back."

When Zac leaned over her again, she saw things she hadn't seen before. This man she'd married and loved, who had his own dark, dangerous side…well, he too was human.

CHAPTER 34

One Year Later

"Happy birthday to you, happy birthday to you!"

Zac was filming Jason's first birthday. Today was just for their two families, his and Sean's, and tomorrow would be for all their friends. Diane had her shoulder-length hair pinned back. This was the first time Zac had ever known her to let her hair grow from the short cop cut she'd always had, but there was a softness about her now that had never been part of her before. She was allowing herself to look like a woman, his woman.

The white cake she'd made was lopsided, two layers, with one candle lit. She'd spent all morning making it even though she knew Zac could have done it faster and better than she could. She wasn't much of a cook, never had been, but this was her baby's first birthday, and even Zac couldn't and wouldn't take this from her.

"Jason, over here. Look up here, bud. You too, Sophia." Sean was filming with his cell phone on the other side of the table, where Annie was sitting in a chair, her long dark hair tied back in a ponytail, a tiny scar above her brow. She was holding their daughter, who was small for her age, with downy dark hair and a smile that lit up her face just like her mother's. She was still so small, being premature, but was doing surprisingly well. She was mesmerized by her own chocolate cake, which Annie had made.

Jason, his boy, had the same round cheeks as his mother, but the way he moved was going to be just like his father, a tough guy. Zac had teased Diane that he had his father's looks, too.

"Come on, blow out the candles!" Zac laughed as Diane and Annie stepped in to help their babies. "Yay!"

Everyone clapped as Jason put his hand into the middle of the sticky icing, pulled out a glob, and shoved it in his mouth. Sophia watched, her lovely dark eyes wide, and Annie scooped some chocolate icing out for her.

"Zac, Sean, put the cameras down and grab some plates," Diane said. She lifted the candle from the cake, then licked off the icing.

"Hey, grab a couple beers, too," Sean said as he tucked his phone back in his jeans pocket and then lifted his baby girl from Annie's lap. He helped Annie from her chair. She still had a limp, but she was doing well after spending three weeks in the hospital and a month recuperating, followed by a lot of physio. At least she no longer had a brace on her leg. Baby Sophia had spent three weeks in the hospital with Annie but had been taken off the respirator after five days. They'd watched her closely, giving her steroids, and she'd rallied. As soon as Annie and Sophia had been discharged, Zac had wondered whether Sean would let them out of his sight for long.

"So I heard it was official this morning," Sean said, carrying Sophia in his arms. She was wearing a pink dress and white socks on her tiny little feet.

"Turned in her badge and gun, officially retired," Zac replied. He would never admit to anyone that he'd worried

Diane would decide to go back to work. He'd seen her struggle watching him go out the door to work, to a crime scene, but he also saw the joy in her face at being with their baby, raising him. It had taken a lot of waiting and patience on his part, giving her the space she needed to make the decision he wanted her to make.

"So how did you twist her arm?" Sean asked.

Zac looked back at his friend and said, "Just by loving her, giving her time, and trusting she'd make the right choice. What about Annie?"

Sean grinned and faced his wife, who was cutting into the cake and laughing over something Diane had said. "Happy, healthy," he replied. "And she wants more kids."

Turn the page for a sneak peek of
*DON'T STOP ME the first book in a brand new series, THE
MCCABE BROTHERS*
Available in eBook, paperback & audio

— "Eckhart has a new series that is definitely worth the read. The queen of the family saga started this series with a spin off of her wildly successful Friessen series."From a Readers' Favorite award—winning author and "queen of the family saga"

—"Another compelling story of profiling and love that will keep you intrigued until the end!"

CAROL C., AMAZON CUSTOMER

—"Featuring a story that could be ripped from the headlines, Eckhart uses her great storytelling ability to craft dynamic, well rounded characters and a well written story." Aherman, Reviewer

The first book in the McCabe Brothers, a spinoff of the big family romance series The Friessens from New York Times & USA Today bestselling Author Lorhainne Eckhart.

Fifteen years ago, Vic McCabe was headed down a one-way road to destruction with the love of his life. But then the unthinkable happened, a mistake that changed their lives forever.

Successful billionaire contractor Vic McCabe is a man every woman wants, but he gives his heart to no one. However, one day a reporter shows up, asking questions about a past he's buried, a mistake he made fifteen years ago that could destroy his future and that of the woman he's tried to forget.

After evidence surfaces, dredging up details of the night that changed his life forever, Vic is forced to seek out the only woman he's ever loved—the woman who has sworn to hate him forever.

DON'T STOP ME
CHAPTER 1

There were times memories would come out of nowhere and hold him still for a moment as if he were a hostage. If he were ever to tell anyone about his fears, about the events he still couldn't believe he'd survived unscathed…well, he knew no one would believe him. He would never share his past, his secrets. They were his—his pain, his hurt, his mistakes. Vic McCabe didn't share with anyone.

He took a moment, brushing back the thin gauze of the curtain and staring into the darkness, seeing only the glow of the street lights in the distance and hearing the rain, which had picked up in intensity. It was late, and every sane person was tucked in for the night, sleeping soundly, maybe dreaming of something that wouldn't give him nightmares and have him sitting up in the dead of night, sweating. No, those people most likely had wives, kids down the hall, and maybe a cat and a dog, a minivan and a small compact. Their biggest worry was whether they could afford to take the kids to Disneyland or skiing in Tahoe for spring break.

It would be an easy life, simple, something Vic could never imagine living.

There was nothing about Vic that fit the mold of

comfortable, simple, or easy. He wasn't made that way. He'd been carved out of the gutter. He wasn't a nice man, and he knew well he should have come with a warning label.

He heard a rustle behind him: the sheets, crisp white cotton, clean and fresh. They would need laundered again now.

"How long have you been awake?" she asked.

He didn't turn around. He didn't have to to picture her running her hands through her long dark hair, sweeping it back from her face. He could hear it, sense it.

"Are you coming back to bed?" There it was in her voice. It was always the same, and again he didn't have to turn to know she'd most likely sat up, pulled up her legs, feeling the awkwardness of the moment.

"I'll call a car for you," he said, but the fact was that he had already sent a text and could see the headlights in the distance down his driveway. The black town car was from the executive service he used when he traveled.

"So that's it?" she said.

He could feel the muscles tighten in his back as he rested his arm on the window frame with the bite of the cool night air on his naked skin. It was welcome in his discomfort.

He heard the rustle again and this time turned only when the bedside lamp flickered on. She was lovely, slim and curvy as she pulled on her underwear and awkwardly stepped around the bed to find her dress on the floor. It was purple and white, sleeveless, but it did nothing for him now as he watched her hurry, slipping her feet into black pumps. Her hair was dark and full, the way he liked it, a tangled mess, and her cheeks were round and her lips lush. Her face had already blended into all the nameless faces of the women he'd bedded and tossed away. Her eyes were the wrong shade of brown.

She was staring at him now, watching him with dark smudges under her eyes from the mascara she'd caked on, the shadow on her lids that had fooled him for a moment, an image of someone else. It was always the same, the appreciation for his body, the marks on his back and the tattoo he shared with no one, always the same. He knew women loved his body, every solid hard part of him, but then, he worked at it with running, weights, and hitting the bag in his gym at dawn before he started each day.

It was the same thing each time, the same way. He was now walking across the hardwood floor, reaching for the black robe he had tossed over one of two blue easy chairs. He slid it on and belted it just as the woman's expression became set and distant. Yes, he'd hidden himself from her, and he reached for her jacket, also tossed on the floor, and held it up. She stared up at him for a second and then accepted his help, shoving her arms into the sleeves as he settled it over her shoulders. He stepped back, careful not to touch her again.

"Just give the driver your address and he'll take you home," he said as she stood there again in front of him, close, with the same familiar expectation. She was waiting for a kiss, some gentlemanly gesture after he'd fucked her, but the problem was that he wasn't a gentleman. He was everything bad, everything a mother should warn her daughter to stay away from.

"Can I give you my number?" she asked with dimming hope in her eyes, which he couldn't allow to remain. He had to crush it and slam the door firmly closed so there would be no question in her mind.

"Don't bother," he said.

She took a step to the door and paused for a second. "So you really did mean no names."

Yeah, he really did, and he'd also been clear that he'd never see her again.

ABOUT THE AUTHOR

"Lorhainne Eckhart is one of my go to authors when I want a guaranteed good book. So many twists and turns, but also so much love and such a strong sense of family."

(LORA W., REVIEWER)

New York Times & USA Today bestseller Lorhainne Eckhart is best known for writing Raw Relatable Real Romance where "Morals and family are running themes." As one fan calls her, she is the "Queen of the family saga." (aherman) writing "the ups and downs of what goes on within a family but also with some suspense, angst and of course a bit of romance thrown in for good measure." Follow Lorhainne on Bookbub to receive alerts on New Releases and Sales and join her mailing list at LorhainneEckhart.com for her Monday Blog, all book news, giveaways and FREE reads. With over 120 books, audiobooks, and multiple series published and available at all, retailers now translated into six languages. She is a multiple recipient of the Readers' Favorite Award for Suspense and Romance, and lives in the Pacific Northwest on an island, is the mother of three, her oldest has autism and she is an advocate for never giving up on your dreams.

"Lorhainne Eckhart has this uncanny way of just hitting the spot every time with her books."

(CAROLINE L., REVIEWER)

The O'Connells: *The O'Connells of Livingston, Montana are not your typical family. A riveting collection of stories surrounding the ups and downs of what goes on within a family but also with some suspense, angst and of course a bit of romance thrown in for good measure. "I thought I loved the Friessens, but I absolutely adore the O'Connell's. Each and every book has different genres of stories, but the one thing in common is how she is able to wrap it around the family, which is the heart of each story." (C. Logue)*

The Friessens: *An emotional big family romance series, the Friessen family siblings find their relationships tested, lay their hearts on the line, and discover lasting love! "Lorhainne Eckhart is one of my go to authors when I want a guaranteed good book. So many twists and turns, but also so much love and such a strong sense of family." (Lora W., Reviewer)*

The Parker Sisters: *The Parker Sisters are a close-knit family, and like any other family they have their ups and downs. Eckhart has crafted another intense family drama… "The character development is outstanding, and the emotional investment is high…" (Aherman, Reviewer)*

The McCabe Brothers: *Join the five McCabe siblings on their journeys to the dark and dangerous side of love! An intense, exhilarating collection of romantic thrillers you won't want to miss. — "Eckhart has a new series that is definitely worth the read. The queen of the family saga started this series with a spin-off of her wildly successful Friessen series." From a Readers' Favorite award—winning author and "queen of the family saga" (Aherman)*

Lorhainne loves to hear from her readers! You can connect with me at:

www.LorhainneEckhart.com

lorhainneeckhart.le@gmail.com

ALSO BY LORHAINNE ECKHART

The Outsider Series
The Forgotten Child (Brad and Emily)
A Baby and a Wedding *(An Outsider Series Short)*
Fallen Hero (Andy, Jed, and Diana)
The Awakening (Andy and Laura)
Secrets (Jed and Diana)
Runaway (Andy and Laura)
Overdue *(An Outsider Series Short)*
The Unexpected Storm (Neil and Candy)
The Wedding (Neil and Candy)

The Friessens: A New Beginning
The Deadline (Andy and Laura)
The Price to Love (Neil and Candy)
A Different Kind of Love (Brad and Emily)
A Vow of Love, A Friessen Family Christmas

The Friessens
The Reunion
The Bloodline (Andy & Laura)
The Promise (Diana & Jed)
The Business Plan (Neil & Candy)
The Decision (Brad & Emily)
First Love (Katy)
Family First
Leave the Light On
In the Moment
In the Family
In the Silence
In the Charm

Unexpected Consequences
It Was Always You
The First Time I Saw You
Welcome to My Arms
Welcome to Boston
I'll Always Love You
Ground Rules
A Reason to Breathe
You Are My Everything
Anything For You
The Homecoming
Stay Away From My Daughter
The Bad Boy
A Place of Our Own
The Visitor
All About Devon
Long Past Dawn
How to Heal a Heart
Keep Me In Your Heart

The O'Connells
The Neighbor
The Third Call
The Secret Husband
The Quiet Day
The Commitment
The Missing Father
The Hometown Hero
Justice
The Family Secret
The Fallen O'Connell
The Return of the O'Connells
And The She Was Gone
The Stalker
The O'Connell Family Christmas

The Girl Next Door
Broken Promises
The Gatekeeper
The Hunted

The McCabe Brothers
Don't Stop Me (Vic)
Don't Catch Me (Chase)
Don't Run From Me (Aaron)
Don't Hide From Me (Luc)
Don't Leave Me (Claudia)
Out of Time

A Billy Jo McCabe Mystery
Nothing As it Seems
Hiding in Plain Sight
The Cold Case
The Trap
Above the Law
The Stranger at the Door
The Children
The Last Stand
The Charity
The Sacrifice

The Wilde Brothers
The One (Joe and Margaret)
The Honeymoon, A Wilde Brothers Short
Friendly Fire (Logan and Julia)
Not Quite Married, A Wilde Brothers Short
A Matter of Trust (Ben and Carrie)
The Reckoning, A Wilde Brothers Christmas
Traded (Jake)
Unforgiven (Samuel)
The Holiday Bride

Married in Montana
His Promise
Love's Promise
A Promise of Forever

The Parker Sisters
Thrill of the Chase
The Dating Game
Play Hard to Get
What We Can't Have
Go Your Own Way
A June Wedding

Kate & Walker
One Night
Edge of Night
Last Night

Walk the Right Road Series
The Choice
Lost and Found
Merkaba
Bounty
Blown Away: The Final Chapter
He Came Back

The Saved Series
Saved
Vanished
Captured

Single Titles
Loving Christine